Gail L. Jenner

"Charles E. Boles, aka Black Bart, may not be as famous as Butch Cassidy or other Western outlaws, but his story is no less fascinating. Students of outlaw history will devour this book!"

— Suzanne Lyon, author of *BANDIT INVINCIBLE: BUTCH CASSIDY*

BLACK BART: THE POET BANDIT

Gail L. Jenner & Lou Legerton

Illustrations by Glenn "Lawrence" Harrington
Courtesy the *Paradise Post*

INFINITY
PUBLISHING.COM

ISBN 0-7414-5138-7

Cover image: Glenn Harrington and The Paradise Post.

Published by:

INFINITY
PUBLISHING.COM

1094 New DeHaven Street, Suite 100
West Conshohocken, PA 19428-2713
Info@buybooksontheweb.com
www.buybooksontheweb.com
Toll-free (877) BUY BOOK
Local Phone (610) 941-9999
Fax (610) 941-9959

Printed in the United States of America

Printed on Recycled Paper

Published March 2009

BLACK BART: THE POET BANDIT

Wallace Stegner wrote (from the Foreword of *The Big Sky* by A. B. Guthrie):

"...history is an artifact. It does not exist until it is remembered and written down; and it is not truly remembered or written down until it has been vividly imagined."

So it is with this story, based on six years of tracking the real Charles E. Bowles (Boles) back and forth across the nation, while imagining the events of his life as they might have happened. – GLJ & LL

PROLOGUE

JANUARY 21, 1888

Charles stepped out into the foggy morning and sighed. He knew there'd be a crowd, and he wasn't disappointed. Reporters, in dark suits and heavy coats, were awaiting his appearance.

"Mr. Bolton," called one, raising his pencil, "how does it feel to be a free man?"

Charles took a long, deep breath. "I can't lie, fellows. It feels good."

The reporter nodded. "And you've had enough thieving?"

Charles smiled as he looked around at the blur of eager faces. "Oh, I'm done with Black Bart and my life of crime. For one thing, I've grown a bit deaf and need spectacles. That would present a bit of a problem for a stage bandit, don't you think?"

The men in dark suits laughed.

A second reporter stepped forward. "But what of your literary efforts, Mr. Bolton? Are you through writing poetry, too? You know, our readers enjoyed the verse."

A ripple of good-hearted cheers passed through the crowd.

Charles tapped the brim of the new bowler he'd been given by the warden just this morning. "If I managed a bit of a rhyme," he said, tilting his chin, "like, as not, it might add to my time. It's better left dead, buried alive, filled with lead—but I thank ye for asking, my fine friend."

A round of applause erupted before Charles could continue. "Like I said, sir, I'm done with my life of crime."

"And what about Mr. Hume? Has Wells, Fargo & Company given you any advice?"

"I would hope Mr. Hume is satisfied that justice was served," said Charles. In truth, the Wells, Fargo & Company detective had avoided any contact with him since his incarceration at San Quentin, but Charles knew the man was following his every move. No doubt he'd been disappointed when Charles was given an early release.

"But you've not served your full sentence. It's been reported that Mr. Hume is apoplectic over this turn of events. He says it's a foolhardy gesture."

"Gentlemen," interrupted Charles, "I served my time and did so with no complaints. How can Mr. Hume be anything but satisfied? I'm satisfied," he added, winking at a man near him.

"Here, here!" responded the man warmly.

Suddenly another journalist at the back of the crowd spoke up. "I do believe he questions your contrite heart, Mr. Bolton. After all, you did manage to fool him twenty-eight times. Perhaps even more than that, if all were told?"

Charles tried to capture the man's glance. "I was able to keep Wells, Fargo & Company rather busy, wasn't I?"

Those nearest him nodded.

"But you're not repentant?" came the immediate reply from the back.

"Oh, I have much to repent, as do we all," Charles said, his steady gaze on the reporter who had finally moved into his line of vision. He was handsome, young, and eager. "Therefore," he added, "I would caution that when you take the measure of a man, be sure to take the full measure."

"Does that mean there is something you'd like to add to your story? Our readers are anxious to know what you are about, sir. Why you chose to rob only Wells, Fargo &

Company, for instance."

Charles grimaced. Tell all?

No, he'd not give these men, or anyone, such satisfaction. "May I get back to you?" He faced the rest of the crowd. "For now, I just want a beef steak and a glass of ale."

"He deserves it," returned another man. "Let him pass."

Just then a coach pulled up.

The crowd fell back and gave Charles clear passage even as they scribbled across their notepads. He moved past them, nodding to those closest.

"Good luck, Mr. Bolton."

Charles stopped.

The earnest young journalist had moved to the end of the line of dark suits and his gaze was clear and focused. "Remember, sir, I'd appreciate your story in full, if you ever have a mind to share it. I work for the <u>San Francisco Examiner,</u>" he added. "The name's Randolph Hearst."

CHAPTER 1

EARLY SPRING, 1849

"Ease up, little brother!" Charles tried to push David off, but David had managed to get him by the belt. A knee slammed against his ribs.

"That's for always getting the better of me," said David.

Charles was mad now. He'd had enough games for one day. He doubled his fist and punched his brother in the shoulder. "Ease up."

David shook off the hit. "Not so fast," he boomed, and then pummeled Charles with two quick blows. "I'm gonna finish you off this time."

"You're asking for a real beating."

"Maybe not," returned David with a laugh. "You're the one taking the most hits."

Without giving warning, Charles grabbed David's shirt collar and rolled him onto his back. With everything he could muster, he punched David in the face.

That's when he felt the blow to his own head. He fell with a thud, his eardrum pounding.

When he rolled over, he was looking up into the piercing blue eyes of his father.

John Bowles stood over him, a scowl on his weather-chiseled face. "You think that's funny? Beating up on your brother?"

Charles held his ear, fighting the tears. In nineteen years he had never shed a tear in front of his father.

"Get up." His father's words fell like bricks.

Charles and David both got to their feet, panting.

"It wasn't Charles' fault," began David. He turned to Charles. "I—I"

"I don't care who started it. Charles, however, always finds a way to finish it."

David jumped in. "That's not true. You're wrong."

"A man don't change color, son. It's time you figured that out."

Charles felt the anger rising up in him, gripping him like a vice. He and his father had never seen eye to eye about anything, most of all about him. "Don't bother, David. Nothing will ever change around here."

John Bowles grunted. "That's right. Just like today. It didn't occur to you I could've used a couple more hands down at Harrington's."

"Father —" David began.

"No more." John Bowles held up a hand. "There are chores still to be done. David, bring the cows down. They'll need milking at noon. And Charles?" He turned to study Charles' face before speaking. "Oh, I don't care what you do. You'll only waller the time away anyway."

Charles steadied himself, held himself to the ground under his feet. There was no point in trying to clear up this misunderstanding with Father.

David turned to Charles. "Hey, big brother, I could use some help."

Charles shrugged. "Yeah, okay."

John Bowles released a snicker of contempt. "Huh."

David's face grew red. "You're wrong about Charles."

Charles shook his head. "It doesn't matter. This has been coming for a long time." He turned to his father. "I'll be leaving as soon as I can."

John Bowles glanced from Charles to David with a look

of derision.

David's eyes widened. "You can't leave."

If David only knew how hard this was for him. "Yes, I can. It's easy. Just walk."

John Bowles sneered before stomping off toward the house—a long, rectangular structure that had not seen paint in a decade.

Charles watched his father start up the veranda's brick steps. In that moment, he knew what he would do. Raising his voice, he turned back to David. "I'm headed to California, little brother, to mine for gold."

David whistled. "California? Gold?"

"Yes, gold."

John Bowles pivoted, his steely gaze raking over both young men. "Only an idiot or fool would be so stupid as to think he can dredge gold out of an icy river in some god-forsaken wilderness."

Without waiting for a reply, John Bowles disappeared into the house.

"Hey, big brother, you can't mine gold all alone. You've got to have a partner."

"You can't go," returned Charles. It was enough he would be leaving as the renegade son. "Father needs you. And Ma would never forgive me."

"Father doesn't need anybody. He just wants someone he can bully around. And Ma will understand—eventually." He shoved Charles and laughed. "You're not the only one who dreams about the future. I'm tired of cold winters and back-breaking summers."

"Mining is back-breaking work."

"It's a far cry from barn raising."

"Well, you'll have to tell Ma yourself," said Charles. "And Father. I've served my days in court with him."

David shrugged. "He doesn't frighten me. Let him and

John and Hiram, and whoever else stays, take care of this place." Slapping Charles on the back, he chuckled. "Wait 'til Robert and James hear about this. They'll want to come, too. Damn, what fun!"

Maria McCue Bowles had stepped through the doorway even as her husband pushed past her into the house. Seeing his puffed and red-cheeked anger, she knew better than to ask him what had happened. Besides, she didn't have much sympathy for his temper any more. But she'd heard enough of the bitter exchange to know that what she'd overheard distressed her.

She watched as David moved toward the barn, whistling. With arms wet with perspiration and white with flour, she called to Charles.

He glanced up.

She frowned. It wasn't that she was surprised by Charles' decision to leave. Heaven knew he and John Senior had butted heads for almost twenty years. What lay at the heart of the matter, she'd never figured out. But had her husband become so hard that he'd watch Charles leave without a fight? And would she lose David, as well?

After taking a slow deep breath, Charles came toward her. He placed a boot on the first step and leaned forward. "Seems I've made a decision, Ma. At least it ought to make it easier on everyone."

Maria moved her hands to her hips. "Charley, when are you going to stop making life so impossible? Life is just plain hard work."

"Ma, nothing I ever do pleases him. You know that. Besides, farming and barn settling have never been my idea of making a living."

"No? What is your idea of making a living?"

Charles straightened. "Something that promises adventure. And opportunity. I want to earn money, Ma. Lots of

8

money. But I can't do it here."

"So you're headed to California?"

Charles' smile was suddenly cockeyed, even playful. "Where else?"

Maria felt her pulse quicken. "Stop being ridiculous. You're going nowhere. Chasing gold is as worthless as trying to rope the stars. Besides, your father can't spare you. You owe it to him to stay."

"Owe it to him? Ma, I can't, I won't, spend my life trying to be what he wants me to be. Even roping the stars would be easier than working alongside him."

"Trouble is you're too much alike, but your leaving will split this family like a rotten rail. I suppose David's going?"

Charles' expression grew hard. "I don't know what David or anyone else will choose to do, Ma."

Maria clutched at the folds of her skirt. If two or three of the boys left, what would she do? What would John Senior do? "This will send your father to his grave."

"And that'll be his choice," said Charles.

CHAPTER 2

The Town Square in St. Joseph, Missouri, clamored with noise. Men cursed, horses whinnied, and dogs, racing under and around creaking cart wheels and wagon wheels, barked incessantly. The stench of animals and men, disheveled and disorderly, rose in a heady cloud above the muddy avenue.

"I don't think I've ever seen a place so full of life!" David pointed to a freight wagon being loaded by three black men. Its team of eight mules stood solemnly in their harness. "Have you noticed the number of coloreds and foreigners? I've never seen such a spectacle of people."

"Everyone's off to see the elephant," said Robert. "Just like us."

"Everyone except us," Charles broke in. "We have yet to find a unit to join up with. And we need a team."

"Teams cost ten times what we'd have paid back home," said David. "Some of the animals James and I inspected were little more than carcasses."

"Well, unless you want to drag your own carcass across the desert, I suggest we find a company and some mules soon," Charles quipped.

By week's end, Charles and his three brothers were able to join a small party headed west. Their leader was an ex-soldier and veteran of the Black Hawk War. A big man, Wayne Cross had a sallow complexion and a thin yellow beard. A scar, the length of a middle finger, curled around his left cheek like a twisted hairpin. Boldly he boasted of an encounter with two drunken Indian scouts.

As wagon master, Wayne Cross ordered that wagons be made of seasoned lumber, with beds liberally caulked to make them watertight. He demanded front wheels be as high as back ones and tires be put on with a bolt in each felloe and a nut and screw on each bolt.

He also demanded that everyone carry extra provisions.

Charles read the list aloud. "That means 300 pounds of flour, 150 pounds of cured ham, 150 pounds of bacon, 30 pounds of sugar, 20 pounds of coffee, and 4 pounds of tea, also 2 pounds of cream of tartar, 5 pounds of soda, and 8 pounds of salt. You could make a rhyme out of that," he offered with a smile. "Let's see. Coffee, tea, tartar and salt. A little sugar and ham, perhaps some malt—"

"We don't have money to buy even half that," grumbled Robert. "We'll have to dip into Ma's purse."

Charles frowned. Though Ma had secretly given Robert a stack of notes, she'd said the money was only to be used if they ended up in California with no way home. Charles had said that no one would touch any of it—ever.

"Captain Cross is as nervous as an old biddy," David grumbled.

"Maybe so," said James, "but his word is law. We signed a contract."

"That don't make him God," protested David.

"He's as close as any man'll get for the moment," said Charles. He turned to James. "Take the list to the storekeep. He ought to have everything we need."

Robert frowned. "Well, at least we don't need to buy any more mules. We got four, and Charles. He's stubborn enough to carry us all to California."

At sunrise, on the second day of May, Captain Wayne Cross signaled the wagon train's start with a gunshot. Immediately the neatly trimmed wagons took their places in line. James and Robert were driving the team, and Charles and David were mounted.

In all, twenty wagons peopled by fifty-three men and three women moved out. Reluctantly Wayne Cross had admitted the women, though he'd made it clear that if any complained, they'd be sent back "quick as a starving dog can lick a dish."

Late in the day, Wayne Cross, riding a large dappled gray gelding and looking more like a general than a wagon master, rode up alongside Charles.

Touching the brim of his hat, Charles asked, "Everything satisfactory, Captain?"

"For the moment," said Cross. "We'll make Blue River tonight. That'll be the last chance for anyone who might've forgot something. It happens—" he added, fondling the ends of his sparse, pale beard.

Charles glanced back at the wagon train, wending its way like a many-jointed worm. The ruts of thousands of wagons had already been carved into the land. He only hoped he hadn't waited too long. Perhaps he should have set out when news of the first strike was reported. Had he done that, he wouldn't have his brothers now to worry about.

No matter. He was on his way. And whatever happened, wherever Providence led him, he would not be sorry. California was his land of golden dreams.

It was at the end of the third week that Captain Cross stopped the train midday, his hand held high. "Buffalo! Over the rise."

The call for riders went up immediately. "Get your guns!"

That night there was a great feast. Two loins and hind-quarters, along with humps and tongues, were roasted over spits. The women brought out apple pies made from dried fruit, served up with pitchers of fresh cream, while whisky—which was not permitted on the trail—found its way into the cups of most of the men. As the shanks of meat glistened and sizzled in the firelight, someone broke out a banjo and old man Taggard raised his harmonica.

The men ate and the music played. Suddenly, two men began dancing, then others joined in. Rudolph Heinz and Bobby Rucker, donning scarves, danced with everyone, clicking their heels and shaking their heads. Robert and James rushed in, too, while David and Charles stood back, smiling and clapping to the music. Wayne Cross stayed in the shadows, his hat drawn over his face, but Charles knew the man was watching, on guard, aware of every night sound and movement.

CHAPTER 3

It was a hot afternoon when the exhausted wagon train reached Fort Laramie.

The last two days had been arduous. Leo Seagrave's and Duncan Miles' wagons had to be abandoned after attempts to rebuild their broken axles failed. Worst of all, the Langston boy had been seriously injured in a foolish accident.

He was rushed to the nearest carpenter's shop because the fort's doctor was away. There, a round, dark woman—the carpenter's wife and a seamstress—stitched up the boy's ragged shoulder and arm as best she could. Hopefully he would survive.

"There wasn't much to save," Wayne Cross said when he approached Charles later. He had spotted Charles in the square that served as Laramie's parade ground. "His arm may still have to come off."

"I'm sorry," said Charles.

The captain nodded as he removed his tobacco pouch and pinched off a wad of tightly wound leaves. "It's a wonder the boy didn't bleed to death. God Almighty, you'd athought he'd know better than to stand on a wagon tongue, even if it weren't rollin' fast. I just hope the boy don't die before the doc gets back." He sighed audibly. "Well, I ain't normally a drinkin' man, but tonight I feel the need. See ya, Charles."

Charles nodded. "You take care now, Captain."

David watched Charles walk across the square. His brother seemed more preoccupied than normal. Hands

14

tucked into his pockets, head bowed, he walked as a man with weighty thoughts.

Of course, understanding Charles had never been a simple task. He had always been the black sheep of the Bowles' bunch, even at a young age, aggravating Father until he'd lash out with hand or strap. David had often wondered why Charles just couldn't let things be. Instead, he pushed. And pushed. Mother's impassioned pleas only occasionally saved his brother from a whipping.

He remembered one incident in particular. Charles could not have been more than six or seven years old and he had decided to go to town. Somehow he'd managed to steal a dollar from Mother's chicken money and, without saying a word, took Father's plow horse and rode off. He was caught by Deacon Simmons, hauled home like a trussed pig, and brought face to face with Father. Resolute, Charles did not apologize.

Father beat Charles soundly.

Charles entered the dark, narrow saloon where gray smoke from homemade pipes and hand-rolled cigars hovered like thick haze over still water. Several men from Wayne Cross' wagon train had already found a game of faro, but Charles did not approach them. He preferred to stand and watch, out of the lamps' glow.

It was almost midnight when Charles noticed the big mountain man entering the saloon. Stopping to look around, the stranger's dark eyes flashed brightly. A few minutes later he approached Charles, his swarthy face appearing even darker in the shadows.

Charles recognized him, having heard the myriad of rumors surrounding the mulatto trapper. Jim Beckwourth was as infamous as any outlaw in the West.

The mountain man pressed one leather-clad shoulder to the mud and timbered wall before turning toward Charles. "Humans are intriguing creatures," he said. His black moustache and bearded chin moved only slightly as he

15

spoke.

Surprised by the man's eloquent speech, Charles replied, "I agree."

"I've met all kinds. Most amuse me greatly."

Charles chuckled and nodded, immediately drawn to the man's wry humor.

"You appear to be a worthy adversary," the big man said. "Let me introduce myself. My name is James Beckwourth. Jim to most." He pointed to the nearest table. "Do you play?"

"Occasionally," said Charles, "when it suits me." He held out his hand. "My name is Charles Bowles, lately of New York, headed to California."

"Well," said Beckwourth, "these games are crooked, even the faro. But, if you're daring, how about trying your luck down at the Sioux camp? They play a game not unlike chuck-a-luck. No hidden mirrors or contraptions. You might find it interesting—"

Charles hesitated. Until now the only Indians he'd encountered operated ferries along the rivers or studied the wagons on horseback from a distance. "Why not?"

CHAPTER 4

The Sioux encampment was outside Laramie's main gate. As the two men entered the small village, two braves, one with long white hair, the other tall and lanky, greeted Beckwourth in a foreign tongue. The mountain man responded warmly.

"You speak their language?" asked Charles.

"As a practical matter, I speak many languages. It doesn't take great intelligence."

Charles inclined his head, thinking to disagree, but the mountain man continued on. He stopped when he reached a lodge that was smaller than the rest.

As Charles stepped through the narrow opening, it took a moment for his eyes to focus.

"Sit," said Beckwourth.

Charles dropped to the hide-covered floor and scanned the faces of five women who sat in a ring beside the crackling fire. Four were old, wrinkled and stern. One was young and pretty.

Beckwourth nodded to each one. "These women are as intelligent as their men, so do not underestimate them—ever. And Weasel Woman here knows what money is and what it can buy, so watch her closely."

After Beckwourth explained the rules of the game, Charles reached inside his vest pocket and withdrew several coins. Weasel Woman nodded, satisfied. In front of her sat a small brooch, obviously a trinket won from some other pilgrim. She picked up a small basket and a handful of stones.

"Pay attention," whispered Beckwourth. "She'll shake them up pretty good, but don't let them fall to the floor or you'll lose."

Charles kept his eyes on the edge of the basket, and when the old woman hit the basket against the hides, he reached out and snagged all but one stone. That one fell to the ground with a tiny thump.

Weasel Woman sputtered indignantly.

Beckwourth laughed. "Well done. You got her. Better claim your winnings."

Charles picked up his own coins, then stretched across and picked up the brooch. In the flickering firelight the cut glass shimmered like a rainbow. Suddenly, without thinking, he held the ornament out to the young woman. "For you," he said and smiled.

The young woman blushed as she took the brooch, and Weasel Woman fumed.

"Ha, friend," broke in Beckwourth, "you may have just won an ally but you've likewise made an enemy. I think we best take our leave."

Charles followed Beckwourth out into the black night. "I fear sometimes I take unnecessary chances."

Beckwourth smiled. "A man after my own heart."

All the next day, Charles deliberated over the stories Beckwourth had told him about the trails he'd traveled and the adventures he'd had. That evening he approached his brothers. "I think we ought to join up with Jim Beckwourth."

"The colored fur trapper?" said James. "Why ever for?"

"He's a scoundrel and a heathen," said Robert. "Tells all manner of lies. The men in the saloon were talking about him last night."

David took a sip of coffee. "Beckwourth doesn't have much to recommend him, Charles, aside from the fact that he apparently lived among the Indians for a time."

Charles drew a slow breath. "There is far more to the man than people realize. He knows the country and he's discovered a cutoff into California that would save time."

"Hogwash," returned Robert. "Besides, we signed a contract, remember?"

"We need to make up time," Charles said. "Face it, we've lost a considerable amount of it in the last few days. Captain Cross can't argue with that."

"Well, if we do have problems from here on out, it's gonna be with the Indians, most likely," said David. "That would make having Beckwourth with us an advantage."

Charles nodded. "Yes, it's the better choice. The captain isn't going to leave until the doctor returns, and then only when the boy recovers."

"I don't like switching horses midstream," interrupted Robert.

"Then you boys stay with Cross," snapped Charles. "I'm leaving with Beckwourth at dawn."

"No," said David, turning to Robert and James. "Where Charles goes, we all go."

CHAPTER 5

After cresting the Sierras, Beckwourth's small party found itself at Gibsonville. Charles, David and James were delighted.

Robert had said little since leaving Laramie, even though they had successfully crossed the desert. Beckwourth had been as good as his word, finding grass when there appeared to be none, even surprising them with berries and fish when they thought they'd go hungry. He'd managed to cut days off their journey and they had reached California well before the wagon train could have.

Gibsonville's mining camp swarmed with activity. Groups of men in tattered clothes greeted them; two offered to buy drinks around for all, except Jim.

Robert chuckled at the men's obvious disdain. "Sounds good to me, brothers."

Charles, casting his brother a stern glance, interrupted. "There's work to be done."

"You're sounding rather like Father these days," taunted Robert.

Jim turned to Charles. "Never wise to pass up a free drink," he said, his black eyes sparkling with mischief, "especially if good gentlemen are buying."

One of the miners sputtered and coughed before spitting out a wad of half-chewed tobacco. His companion slapped him on the back, then frowned at the black scout.

"I don't need your permission, Mr. Beckwourth,"

snapped Robert. "I'm getting drunk. I don't care who says no."

Early the next morning, Charles awoke to find Robert still gone. As he built a small cook fire he realized he was angrier than he'd ever been with his brother. "Damn him, anyway," he mumbled.

David surfaced from under his bedroll. "Damn who?"

Charles looked over at his tousled, happy-go-lucky brother. "Robert. He hasn't returned. I imagine he's laying drunk somewhere."

"Ah, he needed to get it off his chest," suggested David, tiptoeing in stocking feet to join Charles by the fire. "It's colder here than I thought," he added, rubbing his hands. "He's just sour he can't complain about Jim any longer. Where is Mr. Beckwourth, anyway?" David scanned the campsite.

"Don't know. He was gone before I got up."

David shrugged. "I'll fix up some biscuits."

Charles nodded. David's biscuits had become a favorite breakfast item and Jim raved over them frequently.

When Beckwourth returned three hours later, he was toting a pair of shovels and a pick axe over one shoulder. Across the other shoulder he carried Robert, whose head bobbed up and down like a rag doll's.

He dropped Robert and the tools to the ground.

Robert moaned, but never moved.

James, who had returned to camp with an armful of freshly chopped wood, rushed over. "Is he all right?"

"Drunk," returned Beckwourth. "And beat up."

David hurried to help James, who was pulling Robert up against a packsaddle. Robert's head flopped back, his mouth dropped open, and his eyes flickered open.

Charles frowned. "Where'd you find him?"

"Face down in a ditch. Looks as if he took some mean

21

punches."

David sighed. "Look at him. I think somebody left him to die."

"More than likely," said Beckwourth. He raised his brows at Charles as if to warn him against Robert's foolishness. "Not an uncommon end for a lot of greenhorns."

It was hours later when Robert came to. He sat up and eyed Charles before rolling over and curling up into a ball on the ground.

David couldn't restrain his curiosity. Shaking him, he plied him with questions. "Come on, what happened to you last night? If Beckwourth hadn't found you, you might have died. Even still, we worried you were gonna pass into oblivion before coming to."

"Go 'way," snarled Robert.

"Not now, not ever. Now sit up and tell us what happened," said David.

"You don't want to know," whispered Robert. Glancing around, he spotted Jim.

"And I ain't saying anymore 'til that nigra is gone."

Jim turned to Charles. "It's time for me to be moving on, anyway, Charles. But you better watch your backsides. A fool is always an easy target."

CHAPTER 6

Days turned into weeks and the Bowles' brothers had little to show for their hard work. Their food stores dwindled and they had to swap two of their mules for basic provisions. Still, Charles refused to let anyone take from Ma's sacred bundle of money.

He only hoped there would never be a reason to do so, but the fear that all would not end up well, nagged at him each night. He'd not thought it would be this hard to scratch out a living.

The weather turned cold and several days of rain made working conditions miserable. With little more than a lean-to to keep them warm, the days and nights grew longer and longer.

On a particularly bitter morning, James, hovering near the fire, suggested moving to Marysville to wait out the winter months. "There's no sense tramping up and down these streams, freezing feet and hands. I've heard tales of men freezing right to their shovels or long toms, not to be found 'til it was too late."

Robert refused. "And what do you think we'll live on? Every fourth man'll be down there. Prices will be as high as they are here. As it is, we don't have money enough to get us through two weeks, let alone two or three months, that is, unless we use some of Mama's cash."

"That's not an option," said Charles.

"Well, moving to Marysville sounds better than freezing," piped David. "The last few days, I can't seem to get warm for more than five minutes at a time. Cold water, cold nights, cold mornings, cold beans."

"But what will we do for money?" Robert demanded.

James looked at David. "Charles can find a few poker games. He's always been lucky at cards and wrestling. Can't be too many around with his skill."

"That's a great plan," David said.

Charles looked around at each of his brothers. He'd not said anything, but as he saw it, the real problem was David. It didn't take much to see that he was growing pale, almost hollow. James, too, looked pretty rough. Robert, on the other hand, was as robust as ever, and as impatient. No wonder he wanted to continue mining through the winter. "We can manage a couple weeks before we decide," he said.

Robert said nothing, but his glance told Charles that he had his own ideas.

Within the week, however, Charles realized that David was suffering from more than cold or deprivation. One morning, when his brother refused to get up, he discovered him huddled over, his face flushed with fever.

"Don't feel so good," David mumbled. He smiled, but his expression was tense.

Charles stifled his fear. Ruffling David's hair, which had grown long and curly, he teased, "You always were the lazy one."

From the other side of the fire, James gave Charles a questioning glance.

Charles shook his head slightly. This was no time to jump to conclusions.

Moments later, Robert, returning from morning ablutions, entered camp with a frown. "Somebody's taken the mule. Else he's wandered away."

Charles cursed. "Didn't you hobble him?"

"I hobbled him," said Robert. "You want to ask me again?"

James frowned. "Likely as not, he's serving as some-one's breakfast or someone's pack horse out of the mountains."

Charles scanned the camp. Except for a half-dozen utensils and tools, there were few items of value left to worry over. "Then that doesn't leave us many choices, does it? We'll start for Marysville—and the sooner the better."

Robert scoffed. "I told you, big brother, I'm not leaving."

"So be it," snapped Charles. There was no point arguing with Robert. He'd obviously made up his mind about staying; besides, his caustic behavior had made his presence almost infuriating. "One less mule to worry over," he added.

Robert curled his fists as he realized the remark was meant for him.

By the end of the day, Robert was gone. With him went Ma's cash bundle.

David shook his head. "I don't believe it. He stole Ma's money?"

"Shouldn't we go after him?" asked James.

Charles shook his head. "He made his choice. We go on without him. Besides, David is going to need a warm bed before much longer. We'll leave for Marysville as soon as we can arrange it."

"But how much dust do we have?" James asked. "Without Ma's—"

"I know," interrupted Charles. "Hopefully there's enough for passage with one of the sutler's wagons. There's no way David's gonna make it on foot."

"I'm tougher than you think," protested David.

"Good," snapped Charles. "I'm counting on it."

Taking their last poke of gold dust, Charles headed to the nearest settlement. Several tent stores and saloons had already been folded up or abandoned, even though a number

25

of hardy miners would remain in the higher elevations.

Charles passed handfuls of men trudging the muddy trail that led south. Weighed down under loads that included coffee pots and tinware, floppy hats, axes, pans and shovels, they hailed him with friendly banter. But no one seemed to know if any sort of wagon would be coming through.

"You can check with Harry Childs," said one old codger. "I do believe he and his partner'll be headed down. They got a supply outfit. He's probably still up at his claim, three miles upstream."

"Thanks, Mister," said Charles. "That's just what we're looking for."

By the time Charles made it back to camp, a heavy rain was falling. Charles found David resting inside the shelter, two blankets wrapped around him, a small fire struggling to burn. James had gone off in search of dry wood.

"I got you passage out of here," said Charles.

"It's about time," murmured David, giving him a thin smile, "for you have no talent as a carpenter. James had to repair the roof three times since the rain began."

Charles shrugged. "Another reason I was better off leaving New York behind."

David's smile disappeared. "Well, more than likely, I should never have left. Right now I'm as useless as tits on a boar."

"Hardly," returned Charles. "You're a far better miner than James or me and a diplomat. You've kept us all from taking punches at each other more than a few times since leaving home."

"I couldn't keep Robert here."

"No one could've done that."

"Well, the way I see it is if we don't take care of each other, who will?"

26

CHAPTER 7

Charles walked, while David rode the rickety supply wagon down the narrow mountain trails under stormy skies. Unfortunately, he grew weaker each passing day.

At the last minute, James and Charles had decided it best that James stay and work their claim, if only to eke out enough gold to keep them supplied through winter. Charles and David took the last of the dust with them, mindful that it must finance their first weeks in town.

After saying good-bye, they agreed to meet in Marysville in six weeks. By then, God willing, David would be well and the trio would decide where to settle in spring.

When the small company reached Marysville, David was taken to the local doctor's office.

The doctor was gone and wouldn't return for days.

"What do you expect?" grumbled his wife. "There's cholera all over these parts, and the only other doctor took off to try his hand at mining. Not much call for real doctoring, unless it's to stop a gunshot wound or say prayers over the dying. And nobody has a dime to spare."

Charles held his tongue. The woman could hardly be blamed for her ill temper, and she was probably correct in her assessment of the conditions her husband faced.

The doctor's wife studied David's drawn face shrewdly. "There is a small boarding house down the road. The widow who keeps it will take you in for practically nothing. That's all I can offer. That and good luck."

That night, as Charles sat on the edge of the cot where David slept fitfully, he recalled his mother's last words before bidding him farewell: "A great fortune depends on luck, son, and a small one on diligence. Why must you jeopardize what is already yours for something grand but dangerous?"

The question, as much as the sadness reflected in her eyes, unnerved him now. Why couldn't he have been content with a smaller fortune? Why had he been so determined to leave everything—and everyone—behind?

He got to his feet. It was impossible to sleep. Pulling on his coat, he slipped outside to the nearly deserted street. Clapboard buildings and roughly-hewn structures were shoved together like handfuls of children's blocks.

It wasn't long before he noted a pair of well-dressed men approaching him. When he stepped aside to let them pass, the first man stopped.

"Another late night stroller?" he asked.

Startled by the man's familiarity, Charles touched the brim of his slouch hat. "Good evening."

"Well, not so. Your face has the long look of worry," returned the first man abruptly. Taller than his companion, he introduced himself as William Forester. "My friend here is John Leavenworth. Can we be of service?"

Charles fumbled for an answer.

"This your first winter in California?" suggested Forester.

Charles hesitated. "Not much to show for it."

"And where's home?"

"New York."

"Ah," remarked Mr. Leavenworth. "I had occasion to visit New York just last year and thought it wonderful farming country."

"Farming country, perhaps," said Charles, "but the winters are severe."

Mr. Leavenworth agreed. "So you like California then?"

Charles sighed. "Until my brother fell ill, I thought California would be the answer to all our problems."

Forester's countenance darkened. "Is your brother here? Has he seen a doctor?"

"Unfortunately, both doctors are away. We'll have to move on."

John Leavenworth glanced at his companion. "William, the packet headed to San Francisco." He turned to Charles. "There are several excellent doctors in San Francisco."

"San Francisco?" stammered Charles.

"Indeed," said William Forester. Slipping his right hand into his coat, he removed a piece of paper and handed it to Charles. "Give this to the captain. The men who were to accompany our party have not yet arrived, and it's a shame to waste the passage."

Charles shook his head. "Gentlemen, I have no money. I can't accept it."

John Leavenworth waved a gloved hand through the air. "I do not expect payment. However, we leave at 7:30 sharp, and the captain is an arrogant scalawag who will leave you high and dry if you are one minute late."

The men then excused themselves with a hurried good-night, leaving Charles to stare after them.

CHAPTER 8

The packet departed two minutes past the half-hour, but Charles and David had arrived early. Tucked into a corner room near the side-wheeler's steam boiler, David rested while Charles made his way back to the main deck.

As the freighter chugged downstream, Charles leaned forward against the crowded rail and studied the changing landscape. Such fine land. No doubt Father would characterize it as California's real gold.

"Ahem. A farmer's keen eye."

Charles turned at the sound of the familiar voice.

John Leavenworth smiled and nodded toward the riverbank.

"I wasn't prepared for the richness of the land," said Charles.

John chuckled. "It isn't many who take note of California's real treasure."

"That was exactly what I imagined my father saying."

"Yes, well, let me introduce my friends."

Noticing two army officers standing off to one side, Charles bowed slightly. "Charles Bowles," he said.

John Leavenworth put a hand on the first man's shoulder and drew him forward. "This is Army Lieutenant William Sherman." Turning slightly, he nodded to the second man, "This is Lieutenant Robert Ord. They are on a mission to secure new mounts for the army post at Monterey. A beautiful city," he added.

Charles smiled. "It's a pleasure, I'm sure."

Mr. Leavenworth explained Charles' mission.

Charles interrupted him. "It's because of Mr. Leavenworth and Mr. Forrester's incredible generosity that we are on our way to San Francisco."

Mr. Leavenworth shrugged. "Life provides challenges enough. One should never ignore another man's ill fortune when he has the power to affect it."

Sherman nodded. "Unfortunately, I fear most of California's argonauts will find their doom rather than their fortune in California."

"Life is a gamble," returned Charles.

Sherman nodded. "True, and I've always been a gambling man."

When Charles returned to their cramped quarters, he found David half-sleeping, but beset by a round of coughing. Pulling out a flask he'd filled with whisky, he urged his brother to take two hearty belts.

"I've become a real burden," David said. "I'm sorry."

Charles repressed the knot in his stomach. "Yes, well, little brother, you always were a skite."

David, flushing with anger, pulled himself to a sitting position and grabbed Charles. "Don't do that. You always do that. I know I'm dying, Charlie. You hear me?"

Stunned, Charles' wrapped his fingers round David's pale, thin ones. "That's nonsensical, pure nonsensical. This fever has you thinking desperate things, that's all."

Exasperated, David leaned back. "Damn you, big brother, you never listen to me, but I'm telling you to listen up now. I'm not going to make it. I feel it in my bones, I know it up here." He placed a trembling finger against his temple. "So you've got to do two things for me." The words exploded like tiny bubbles in the air between them. "First, write Ma. Tell her it wasn't your fault. Tell her I wanted to come to California. Tell her," he hesitated, "I saw the elephant."

Shaking his head, Charles tried to dismiss David's pleas. "You will not die, so stop trying to convince yourself that this is the end. This is just the beginning."

David rolled his head to one side, his once-ruddy cheeks sallow in the dim light. "The second thing is to make peace with Robert."

Charles frowned. "Robert left us, remember?"

David sighed. "Yes, I know, but it's festering inside you like a cancer. And it'll eat at you, just like the bitterness you've always carried for Father."

"Stop this nonsense," said Charles impatiently. "You're too ornery to die. Besides, who'd keep tally of all my sins if you departed? Nah, you've got a long way to go before dying. You hear me? Now rest. And no more foolish blather."

CHAPTER 9

Assisted by John Leavenworth, Charles and David disembarked in the fog-shrouded morning. Lieutenants Sherman and Ord, who had invited the Bowles' brothers to share their buggy once they were on land, waited at the end of the dock.

"Doctor Hyde's office is not far," said Sherman as he helped David into the carriage. "Just up Kearney Street."

"We are grateful," Charles said.

Sherman smiled. "I only pray we've gotten your brother here in time."

Charles nodded. "David is known for his audacity. I'm sure he'll be fine."

Without spending much time in consultation, Doctor Hyde insisted that Charles leave David in his care. "I will give him the best care money can buy."

Charles assured the doctor that payment was not a problem.

But as he made his way through the bustling, bawdy Barbary Coast, Charles wondered where the money would come from. His pockets were as lean as his belly.

He found a hotel pressed between two saloons where a man could sleep cheaply. The room was small, dark, and the bed ticking rough and uncomfortable, but he didn't have to share the space with anyone.

It was dark when a fracas outside wakened him.

Pulling back the shabby curtain strung loosely across the only window, he saw two drunken miners lumbering up the alley. One was waving two large pouches above his head, but, drunker than the first, he floundered and fell against the wall of the hotel. He sank to the mud in a heap.

The first man continued on, unaware that his comrade had fallen.

Suddenly, Charles was moving. He threw his coat over his shoulders and, scrambling down the stairs, located a side entrance. He found the second miner still wallowing in the mud.

Reaching down, Charles slipped an arm around the hefty man. The man took a staggering step forward. They entered the hotel without being seen.

Faced with a hall lined with closed doors, Charles hesitated.

At the same time his companion jerked free. "Hold your taters, Henry," he mumbled. "I got the key here some-wheres."

The man fumbled through his pockets before pulling out an over-sized key.

Charles tried the first door with the key and it turned easily. The big man toppled into the room like an unwieldy sack of grain.

Charles waited to see if anyone would come to the drunk's rescue. When no one did, he pulled the door closed behind him.

Knowing this was crazy, knowing this was an act he'd never thought himself capable of committing, Charles held his breath. If he was going to steal a man's gold, he'd better do it right and not get caught.

It wasn't long before the lusty miner was snoring soundly. Tapping him gently, Charles carefully slipped his hands around the man's beefy middle and untied the leather pouches he seen earlier.

Even more carefully, he stepped back, then opened the door. No one was in sight.

All night Charles lay awake, but no alarms sounded.

At daybreak, dressing quickly, he took the two gold sacks and wrapped them inside his coat. He descended the stairs and casually stepped out into the fog.

It had almost been too easy. And he felt no remorse.

In fact, he felt a surge of complacency. After all, a reasonable crime was a reasonable response, a justifiable action, if it could save the life of another human being.

He hurried to Hyde Street where the doctor met Charles at the door. "I'm sorry," he said, his manner apologetic.

Cold fear trickled down Charles' spine. "Sorry?"

"Advanced pneumonia. Nothing to be done. He died around midnight."

"Midnight? Dead?" A clock chimed in Charles' brain. Midnight? Just as he had stealthily guided the drunk to his room and taken his gold?

The doctor reached out. "Please, come in. There's no sense in punishing yourself. This is rough country. You knew that before setting out, surely."

As Charles followed him into the dimly-lit office, his mind reeled with strange remembrances: how Father had always said Charles would come to no good, how Mother had begged him not to take his brothers off into the wilderness, how Father had refused to say good-bye the day they left Plessis.

They knew, even then, that Charles would lead his brothers to disaster.

CHAPTER 10

Saying farewell to David at the cemetery was the hardest moment Charles had ever experienced. For what must have been an hour, he stood staring at the dirt now humped up over his grave. The gravedigger had offered him his condolences, but aside from that, there had been no song, no scripture, no tears. Nothing to mark the day or year, only a miserly wooden cross he'd bought from a ragged merchant at the bottom of the hill.

"Forgive me," he whispered, dropping to one knee and scooping up a handful of cold earth. "You warned me and I didn't listen. I didn't want to listen."

He slipped his free hand into his pants' pocket and removed a kerchief. Shaking it open, he gently dropped the wet clump into the center of it, refolded it over and over, then slipped it back into his pants' pocket.

It would be all he could offer his family.

Suddenly, a niggling thought took hold and he fingered the gold pouches he'd laced to his belt. Estimating the distance between the tip of his boot and the head of David's grave, he began digging a hole near David's feet. The dirt felt wet and cold under his fingernails, but he didn't quit until he had a hole the size of a 5-lb. sack of flour. "Well, little brother, once again you'll be the one doing the looking after." He dropped the gold into the hole.

When all was done, he brushed the dirt off his hands. "In a year, not longer, I'll be back. Till then—well, till then."

CHAPTER 11

It was back in Marysville that Charles ran into Captain Wayne Cross.

Spotting him from a distance, Charles crossed the muddy, crowded street to greet him. "Hallo, sir!"

The big man, his yellow beard neatly trimmed and groomed, smiled as he recognized him, even with beard and moustache. "I see you made it after all."

"As did you. And the Langford boy? Did he make it?"

The question mark on the captain's cheek turned down. "For a time. A sad twist of events, though. Missus Langford, his mother? She up an' died when cholera hit us. Then the boy fell ill and died, too, and the old man buried them both. We left him in one of the Mormon camps, half-crazed with grief."

Charles shook his head as the grief he'd been stifling each day since leaving San Francisco washed over him. He glanced away, steeling himself against the captain's critical eye.

"So tell me. Beckwourth didn't run out on you, did he? And you struck it rich?"

Charles forced himself to smile. "Hardly."

"But you're here. And, as it happens," Captain Cross interjected, "I just seen your colored friend this mornin'. He was settin' outside the newspaper office."

More grateful than he could say, Charles thanked the captain once more for his able leadership, then excused himself. He had never wanted to see an old friend more than at this moment.

The mulatto trapper was still seated outside the newspaper office.

"Well, if it's not the gold digger," chuckled Jim, dropping his feet to the plank walkway. He'd caught sight of Charles as soon as he'd rounded the street corner, but he waited to see what his old acquaintance was up to. He stood and extended his right hand. "I thought you were panning somewhere up around Gibsonville, but, from the disparaging look of you, I'd wager you haven't found your fortune yet."

Charles took the big man's outstretched hand. "You're right."

Jim looked him over carefully. There was more wrong than right in Charles' expression.

Charles drew close. "We had some trouble."

Beckwourth frowned. He liked Charles more than most of the pilgrims he'd met and he could see that the man was ailing. "What kind of trouble?"

Charles took a deep breath. "David is dead. I buried him in San Francisco."

Beckwourth didn't know what to say. He'd seen how close the brothers had been. "I am sorry, Charles. Terribly sorry."

Charles nodded. There was appreciation in his expression.

Jim scratched at his chin whiskers before venturing on. "And James and Robert?"

Charles squinted as he shrugged. "That's the kicker. I left James with the gear, but Robert—he left us high and dry weeks ago. Thought maybe you might have seen him."

"Wish I could say yes, but then, I've only been in town a few days. I've been working on establishing the outpost I told you about."

"Good for you, Jim." Charles smiled suddenly. "Well, I haven't much time before winter really settles in. I need to find James."

"And most of the miners will be looking for a place to dry out soon. Maybe you ought to roll out your bed and wait until spring. James will surely come down if you don't make it back."

Charles shook his head. "No, I owe it to him to get back as soon as possible."

"Are you saying you need a good guide?"

"Are you asking?"

Jim chuckled. He'd forgotten how easy it had been to befriend Charles. "Well, I thought I might head back up to Bidwell Bar myself. Would that be anywhere near to where you left James?"

"Not far. Anyway, I'd like the company," Charles said. "It couldn't get any better."

Beckwourth smiled. "Come morning?"

"Daybreak."

Beckwourth and Charles made good time, and it was as they turned upriver several days later that they learned of James Bowles' whereabouts. He'd stopped at several miners' cabins along the way.

News in this territory traveled quickly.

"Come with me," Charles insisted, when Jim said he'd be on his way. "James would be glad to see you."

Beckwourth shook his head. "I'm not one to dirty up the water too many times. No doubt I added to Robert's general disenchantment and James will not have forgotten that."

"If that's true, it'd disappoint me."

"Every man has reasons for doing the things he does, Charles, and well you know it. Far be it for me to judge another man's actions."

Charles thanked Beckwourth for his company. "And lest you forgot," he added, pulling out the pouch he'd carried under his belt since leaving San Francisco, "I have at least a portion of the money we still owe you."

"Indeed? Well, then, you've been making do after all."

"More like scratching, but debt is a bad companion."

"Ah, better old debts than old grudges."

Charles approached James' campsite, just as the dying shadow of the pale sun spilled out across a rocky ledge lining the riverbank below. Catching a glimpse of his brother, he raised a hand over his head in greeting, then led Jim's tired mule down the trail. Jim had refused to take the animal with him, saying he was as worthless as an old dog with three legs.

"Charles!" James hollered, his heavy beard and moustache turning up in a grin. "Where's David?"

Hesitating, Charles dropped the lead rope.

"Where's David?" James repeated.

Charles took a deep breath and released it, his words spilling out around him. "We didn't make it in time, James."

"What do you mean, 'didn't make it in time?'"

Charles stepped around to yank on the mule's lead rope. He led the animal down to the ramshackle camp that James had constructed. It was not much more of a shelter than their first.

Without looking back, he stepped around to the side of the mule and tugged on the pack. It fell to the earth, its heavy thud the only sound echoing in the deadly silence enveloping them. "Just what I said. He didn't make it." He turned and glared at James. "David died of pneumonia. He's dead and buried."

James blinked as his mouth worked open and close, but no response came out. Then, without warning, he raised his fist and pummeled Charles.

CHAPTER 12

The Bowles' brothers' homecoming was not a pleasant one. Arriving in Plessis in early spring, James and Charles hired a rig and driver to take them home.

"They can't hold it against you forever," James said, as the driver pulled up in front of the familiar gate. "I've forgiven you, for land's sake."

Charles said nothing. He was grateful his brother had finally forgiven him, but he'd been there, after all. He'd seen how tough conditions were. And he'd eagerly followed him west, too, while their parents had warned them that the journey would be folly.

It was Maria who saw them first. Opening the door, she stepped out onto the back stoop, her hand cupping her eyes to get a clearer look. "Charles? James?"

James, seeing her standing there, waiting patiently, dashed up the walk and threw his arms around her. "Oh, Ma, it's good to be home."

Maria stepped back and studied him critically. "You've lost weight. Same as Robert."

"Robert?" Charles, who still stood at the end of the walk, stepped forward cautiously.

"He came home weeks ago," she said, her glance taking in Charles' weather-worn face. "Said he just wasn't cut out for fortune hunting. He's out with your pa now, rebuilding Harrison's barn that blew down in the last storm. Four barns in all went down, which has been a blessing to this family, I can tell you."

Charles nodded, relief flooding through him. At least he

wouldn't have to conjure up some kind of an explanation as to where Robert had ended up.

"But where's David? Don't tell me he's still digging up half of California?"

James, one arm firmly wrapped around his mother's shoulder, tipped his head and whispered, "He got sick, Ma. Real sick. Pneumonia."

Maria steeled herself as she broke free of James' embrace. "What are you saying?" Her eyes narrowed as she turned toward Charles. "What are you saying?"

The disparaging look in his mother's eyes tore at his gut even more than the sight of David's dead body. "Ma," he whispered, "I took him down to San Francisco to see a doctor, but it was too late."

Maria sucked in her breath as she clenched her fists.

He wished she'd take a swing at him, just as James had done.

"So now you return home? With your tail tucked between your legs? Did you think I'd be waiting for you, with open arms, as if all was well?" Tears were finding their way down her sallow cheeks.

James glanced at Charles before turning his own tear-streaked face to her. "Ma, we did what we could. Honest. He went so fast."

She dismissed him with an impatient wave. "It was you," she said, facing Charles, "you and your foolishness that led David to his grave. God have mercy on your soul. And I suppose you expect your father to forgive you, as well? Don't count on it."

Stunned by his mother's callousness, Charles swung around and headed back down the stone path. For once, he was truly beaten.

Unequivocally beaten.

How could he have been so stupid as to think Mother, or Father, would welcome him home?

"Charles!" James' voice was shrill, almost desperate, but Charles did not stop or turn around. It wasn't James' fault. Ma was right. Charles was the one who was to blame for everything gone wrong.

Without responding, without giving his mother or brother a second glance, he pushed open the front gate, then slammed it shut.

"Charles!" James called out once more. "Come back!"

Charles broke into a run.

If he never went home again, it would be too soon.

CHAPTER 13

Back in California, Charles walked and worked his way through a number of mining towns, from Marysville to Bangor, Slipper Ford to Oroville, Boston Ranch to Granite Basin. But his proverbial good luck had turned sour, and the hope that had been California was dead, just like David.

Still, he couldn't leave. There was nothing to return home to, and there was nothing to replace the dream he'd carried for so long.

So it was on a blustery May morning that he headed back to San Francisco. He needed to start over, somewhere, which meant he needed cash. He'd dig up the rest of the buried purse, then come up with a plan.

It was a week later, while seated at a small corner table in a San Francisco café, that Charles noticed two police officers at a nearby table deep in conversation.

The younger officer, tall and angular, was laughing. "I tell you, these three trappers were the most god-awful varmints I ever smelled. Pie-eyed, to boot. Rattling on about high stakes up in Petaluma, games where a man could win a thousand dollars in less time than it takes to cut up a beef."

"These games can't be any richer than games played anywhere," returned the second officer. He was a bulky man with wiry red hair and a long thin moustache. "If I were you, I wouldn't try winning back the money you've already lost. You're a poor excuse of a poker player, Sam, and you'd do better to stay away from faro or poker."

"I'm telling you, the old codger said these Petaluma

games are easy pickings. I can't help but win back some of my money. After that, I swear I'm not going near a poker table again."

The red-haired man shook his head. "The captain will skin you alive—"

Charles smiled in spite of himself. Perhaps his luck was changing.

The journey to Petaluma gave Charles plenty of time to evaluate his course of action. He shook off the second thoughts he'd struggled through and turned his attention to studying the passing landscape. Details were what made a plan fail-safe. He noted tree stumps and burned-out trees, rocky outcroppings, and more; there was no telling when or where he might need a good hiding place.

He checked into the Stony Point Inn at dusk, then made his way to the downstairs saloon. A tow-headed bartender greeted him. With a pistol stuffed into his green-striped trousers, a brilliant red silk vest and lacey black suspenders, he appeared more as a circus performer than a barkeep.

Charles stepped forward and ordered a beer, then, looking past the handfuls of ruffian-looking miners, noted two faro tables where fur trappers and gamblers were seated.

These must be the gamblers he'd heard about.

It wasn't long before Charles fell into conversation with a pair of miners. One was decidedly down on his luck, while the other, who introduced himself as Ben, began bragging about a recent strike he'd made. He'd also just doubled his purse in a poker game.

Charles congratulated him. Pleased with the attention, Ben ordered a bottle of whisky and three glasses. Charles only sipped at his, his mind more on the activity around him than on the tedious tales Ben spun. But the information could prove useful so he let the man dribble on.

It was well past midnight when the first man excused himself. "I'm on my way come morning," he announced. He reached for his hat. "And if my luck don't change, I'll be headed back home. I left a wife in Illinois," he added.

Ben laughed. "You're a fool, Henry. There's enough gold in California to make us all rich." He wiped his mouth with the sleeve of his coat.

Charles bid Henry a good night and a good journey, then refilled Ben's glass carefully. "So, your claim's not far from here?"

"I ain't about to tell you," warned Ben, raising his furry eyebrows. "But I will tell you that I'll be a rich man in short order."

"You keep saying that," returned Charles, "but I haven't seen much in the way of proof."

Ben reached into his coat and pulled out a pouch. He looked around. "And this ain't the only dust I got," he whispered. "But I ain't no fool. I don't plan on sharing with anyone." He belched as if to emphasize the seriousness of his intent. Then he shoved the pouch back into his coat pocket and got to his feet.

Charles, pushing back his own chair, shrugged. "I won't pretend not to be interested, but I commend your good sense. Besides, it's time I retired."

"Me, too," mumbled Ben. "And I ain't normally a drinking man. It can cost you if you imbibe too freely."

"Indeed," Charles said.

Ben laughed. "Tonight I was celebrating."

"Yes, well," Charles said as the two men entered the foyer of the inn, "I'm up the stairs."

"I'm down the hall." Ben staggered forward until he came to the first door on the right. He seemed to study it a good while, then slid the key into the lock. It turned easily.

Charles caught him by the shoulder and one arm.

The man shrugged him away. "Thank you and good night," he said, turning to peer down at Charles. "What did you say your name was, anyway?"

Charles smiled slowly. "Howard J. Boling."

As soon as Ben's door was closed, Charles smiled. It hadn't been much of a trick to wheedle the pouch out of Ben's over-sized coat, and by the weight and size of the poke, he knew he'd managed to wrangle more than enough money to keep him for a good spell.

He pushed aside any sense of remorse. Hadn't the old fool contended that this was just a sampling of his new-found wealth? That being said, he had nothing much to lose.

Climbing the stairs to his room, Charles contemplated on ways to spend the money. Should he stay in California? Or head east, to Illinois, where his sister Sarah and husband John lived? They'd begged him for years to come and visit, and he'd never done it.

Perhaps now was the time.

CHAPTER 14

Charles enjoyed working alongside John even if it meant getting his hands dirty. The two men talked about California and about gold; it was clear John had dreams of seeking his own fortune. Charles, however, refrained from encouraging his brother-in-law to leave Illinois and go west. He had erred once too often when he'd agreed to take his own brothers.

As one week turned into two, Charles wondered what his next step should be. He avoided most of the social engagements Sarah contrived on his behalf, knowing she had decided he needed a mate.

But Charles agreed to attend the harvest picnic and social to be held at the Macon County fairgrounds on the following Saturday. The festivities would continue all day and well into the evening and featured a wrestling match. That, decided Charles, might well be worth pursuing. A sizeable purse would be put up for each championship match.

"With your skill in wrestling," John assured him, "you should win easily."

"But I haven't done any since leaving New York."

"You're fit as a fiddle," said John.

Sitting in the back of the wagon with young Charlie and Albert, Charles enjoyed the ride into Decatur. The road was crowded with rigs, and John and Sarah called out to a number of people as they rolled along.

"See there?" said Sarah excitedly. "That's the Merry-

50

man's wagon just ahead of us and with them is Mr. Merryman's niece, Miss Mary Elizabeth Johnson. She's visiting from Belleview, Illinois."

Charles glanced over at the freight wagon being pulled by two blacks. "Is that why you begged me to come to this picnic, sister?" He didn't add that he had already noticed the smiling Miss Mary Elizabeth Johnson.

"Could be," said Sarah, feigning ignorance. "Isn't it about time you made the acquaintance of some eligible young lady? You might otherwise die a grumpy old bachelor."

John nudged Sarah. "You're incorrigible, dear. Charles is far from being old. Grumpy, perhaps, but not old."

They all laughed.

By noon, dozens of wagons and carriages had arrived and people were spread out across the parade grounds. Blankets were unrolled and parasols unfolded. As women set out food, men wandered from site to site, stopping to visit or accept drinks and a smoke. The children ran off, their laughter and shouts resounding across the parade grounds.

After lunching, Charles and John wandered over to a ribboned area where two contestants had begun the wrestling tournament. John leaned toward Charles and whispered, "Neither of these fellows is a match for you."

"I don't know, John. It's been a long time since I've taken on a real opponent."

"I've seen you wrestle, Charles," returned John. "Believe me, whoever you're pitted against will have his hands full."

The match took three-quarters of an hour but when it was over, the crowd burst into applause. The winner smiled and raised his arms in victory, then challenged others to step forward.

After a few minutes of hushed silence, a large, curly-haired man stepped forward. Pulling off his shirt and boots, he jumped into the circle. "Try me," he taunted.

John nudged Charles. "Let's get you ready. These fools are just showing off."

Leading Charles to where a bespectacled man sat amidst a small crowd of men, John asked, "Is this where we sign up?"

The man nodded.

"Now, gentlemen," continued John, "this is Charles Bowles. He's here to challenge anyone to a real match. I'd suggest you lay your bets on him; he's the best."

"He don't look like much," mumbled one man as he moved in to study Charles more closely. "I may have to lay money on his opponent."

John smiled. "And I warrant, you'll be sorry."

By the time Charles and Malcolm Haddaway entered the ring twenty minutes later, the crowd had swelled. Haddaway was favored to win handsomely, which meant that if Charles could take him, he'd win a sizeable purse.

The match lasted less than twenty minutes, and in spite of Malcolm's size, Charles took him down easily. After the last round, the official declared Charles the winner. Smiling, Charles offered his hand to Malcolm Haddaway.

John raised his voice above the mumbling crowd. "I told you to lay your bets on Charles. He's fast and he's able."

Charles and John made a handsome profit that afternoon, and Charles, shaking his pouch of coins above Charlie and Albert's heads, chuckled, "How about some penny candy to celebrate?"

The boys cheered and Sarah sighed.

"You will spoil them," she said, raising her eyebrows.

"Good," returned Charles.

The sudden appearance of Mary Elizabeth Johnson caused Charles to nearly stumble. On the arm of her uncle, she approached gingerly.

Mr. Merryman spoke first. "John, you must introduce us. I never enjoyed a match as much as that one."

John shook his hand, then turned to introduce Charles. "Charles is Sarah's brother, lately of California. Charles, this is our neighbor and friend, Ernest Merryman, and his niece, Miss Mary Elizabeth Johnson."

Charles turned to Mary. "I apologize for my ragged appearance."

"Not at all," whispered Mary. "I rather enjoyed the bout. Uncle couldn't keep still and I found myself cheering, too."

"I was just lucky. Very lucky," Charles added, with a smile.

Sarah, stepping over to Charles, placed her gloved hand on his shoulder. "My brother is modest. He is by far the cleverest and most intelligent of my father's children. The rest of us look to him continually for counsel."

Mary Elizabeth turned her blue eyes on Charles, and he felt the immediate intensity of her approval.

CHAPTER 15

Charles glanced at his pocket watch.

John, moving to his elbow, patted him on the shoulder. "It'll be over in a few minutes." He chuckled. "I remember how nervous I was before my wedding."

Charles grimaced. "I suppose every groom is fit to be tied."

"I warrant you, 'tis true," returned John. "But you've made a good choice, Charles."

Charles brushed the lapels of his new jacket, a gift from Sarah and John. "I have every intention of paying you back for this coat. It was enough to have you here. You didn't need to give me such a gift."

John waved a hand irritably through the air. "I never paid you for the work you did around the place. Besides, we couldn't have you getting married in that dusty old frock you call a coat. Sarah would have been mortified."

"Well, I suppose I'll put it to good use. A school master needs to look the part."   "Indeed you do. But a bit green around the gills, I think."

"Only anxious to be done with all this ceremony."

The two men entered the dim chapel a few minutes later.

Mary Elizabeth Johnson, her face hidden under layers of delicate lace, entered the chapel on the arm of her father. He guided her forward, his gaze fixed on Charles, his long craggy nose reminding Charles of a shore bird's sharp, pointed bill. His eyes pierced the pale light that filled the chamber, sending a shiver down Charles' spine.

But when Mary Elizabeth raised her veiled head, Charles relaxed. Her lips curved up in a sweet smile and tears shimmered in her eyes. He reached out to take her hand, and it didn't matter that her father released it reluctantly.

It was a week later that Mary Elizabeth and Charles left Belleview for Forsythe, Illinois. Mrs. Johnson cried inconsolably as Charles ushered his bride down the veranda steps to the carriage he'd borrowed for their journey.

Mr. Johnson, his expression dark but resolute, shook hands briefly with Charles. "I expect you to write now and again," he said to Mary Elizabeth. "Your mother will want to know how you are getting on."

"Of course, Father," Mary whispered.

He stepped back, clearing his throat. "I expect you to do right by your husband. Your allegiance is important."

She reached out and took Charles' hand in her own. "Of course," she whispered.

Her smile was all the confirmation a father needed. "Then, God-speed. We wish you well." He turned to his wife. "Give them your blessing."

Mrs. Johnson tearfully kissed Charles and Mary Elizabeth goodbye.

It seemed unnatural to have a woman beside him, thought Charles as he urged the buggy horse forward. Keenly aware of his new wife's every movement, the rustle of her petticoats, the scent of her hair and skin, he wished they didn't have such a long day's journey before stopping to rest.

As he felt Mary Elizabeth's fingers on his arm, he turned. She was so eager to please, he wondered how he could ever want for more.

Life as a schoolmaster, however, Charles soon found dull and taxing. Only the thought of coming home to Mary

Elizabeth each night made the days worth the effort.

Charles' students were twenty-three rowdy, poorly-mannered children, some with no ability to cipher or read and others with no interest in learning to do so. They quarreled when he left the room, and several times a day, he had to break up fights between the older boys.

There were few materials and the slates the children used were either broken or worn. With little wood on hand, and the stove in need of repair, the room was damp and cold. The smallest children suffered the most since they sat nearest the blackboard where little heat radiated. He petitioned the minister and the mayor for help, but both refused to provide any assistance; the school had always managed to run on the few dollars doled out, they said, and he'd do well to remember that.

Irritated, Charles returned home and confided in Mary Elizabeth that being a schoolmaster was a challenge he feared he was not up to taking on.

"Now, Charles," she said, as she reached out to touch him, "I'm sure the school will, in time, provide what's needed. How could they not, when they see what you bring to their children? Do not be humble. You are magnificent when you set your mind to something."

She smiled, but the smile seemed to hide some warning, and he suddenly realized how much his young wife was counting on his performance.

He was deeply disappointed. This was not how he had intended to live his life.

CHAPTER 16

It was in the first week of January, 1855, that Mary Elizabeth announced that she was expecting a child. Her joy was hard to contain.

"That's wonderful," Charles replied, but, suddenly overwhelmed by the prospect of another person to feed and clothe, he didn't know if he were truly pleased at all. He feigned excitement as he took Mary Elizabeth into his arms.

Unfortunately, she grew weak with her pregnancy and this alarmed Charles. Remorseful, he brought her flowers and tried to console her when she began to find it impossible to rise each morning.

"I can prepare my own breakfast," he said.

"It's my responsibility," she whispered. Tears glistened beneath her lashes and he pressed her hands to his chest.

"Your responsibility is to take care of yourself. Perhaps I should fetch the doctor."

"No, there's nothing he can do," Mary said, her cheeks flushed, her lips parted. "This will pass. It will."

"Then give yourself time. Do not chastise yourself or think that I'm growing impatient. Your health is far more important than my discomfort." Charles leaned over and kissed her lightly.

"Your moustache tickles," she murmured, her eyes softening.

"I thought you liked it."

"I do. It gives you an air of importance. A good quality in a schoolmaster."

He repressed his frown. "Rest," he said and he stood up and straightened his coat. How could he tell her how much he hated the sound of that word?

She sighed and closed her eyes. "It's easy to rest when you look so dashing."

Charles chuckled, wishing he could feel what he knew she wanted him to feel, but he feared he was doomed to disappoint his lovely young wife.

Just as he'd disappointed the rest of his family.

If only I were a better man, he thought. He closed the door to the bedroom and headed out to the front porch.

Clouds rolled across the horizon and threatened rain.

If I were a drinking man, he thought, I suspect this would be the moment when I dug up the bottle and started in.

CHAPTER 17

Their daughter was born on April 26, after a long and hard delivery. Mary Elizabeth raised her exhausted eyes to Charles. "She's perfect," she whispered.

He picked up the child, its tiny red face hardly visible beneath the layers of fabric in which the midwife had swaddled her.

"What shall we name her?"

"Anything you'd like," Charles said.

"Are you disappointed that she's not a boy?"

"A son would be wonderful," chided Charles, "but every man needs a daughter."

Mary Elizabeth smiled and turned to the midwife. "I told you my husband was a real gentleman."

The midwife eyed Charles. "Yes, you did. And it looks to be so. Not every husband is as gracious."

The baby squirmed. Charles wondered if she'd be a fussy baby, a demanding child, a strong-willed woman. He was well used to strong-willed women.

"She wants to suckle," smiled Mary Elizabeth. "She knows what she wants."

Charles placed the child in her arms. "I was afraid of that."

"Would you have it any other way?" As Mary Elizabeth brought the child up to her breast, she asked, "How about Ida for a name?"

"Ida, it is," he said, backing up. In spite of the fact that his mother had birthed ten children, she'd never allowed any of them to witness the ignoble act of suckling.

He escaped to the front room and the fire that blazed there. He'd tried to keep the place as warm as he could, but the dampness seemed to permeate the thin walls in spite of the heat he'd kindled.

He pulled the rocking chair closer to the fire.

He knew he would have to write Mary Elizabeth's folks and Sarah and John with the news, though there would be no opportunity to deliver it for many days, but did he also owe his mother and father a letter?

Sarah had been the one to announce his move to Illinois and his nuptials, saying the family deserved his attention, in spite of all that had happened.

He'd not argued with his sister, but he'd refrained from making any personal contact.

Ironically, he knew Father would like Mary Elizabeth. He'd like her strong character. Maybe even wonder what possessed her to marry a man like his son.

Ida grew plump and curly-haired. Her laughing eyes were china blue, the color, declared Mary Elizabeth, of Charles' eyes. But he saw nothing of himself in her. From all recollection, he'd been a fussy and irritable child, but she was delightful and enchanting and seemed to keep Mary Elizabeth busy and happy.

For Charles, the new term at school took up most of his time and all of his patience. Enrollment had risen as folks learned of the new schoolmaster. But there were still too few books and fewer desks; the children squeezed together along roughly-hewn boards that served as benches.

Most days Charles returned home, reluctant to discuss the disdain and loneliness he harbored. He didn't want to worry Mary Elizabeth when there was nothing he could do about their situation.

But Ida was only eighteen months old when Mary

Elizabeth announced that another child would be coming in late spring or early summer. Rocking beside the fire with the sleeping Ida in her arms, she kept her eyes fixed on the glowing embers.

"Your health," Charles said, putting aside the book he'd been reading. "You're not strong enough."

"What's to be is God's will," Mary Elizabeth responded. "Besides, every man needs a son. And I promise not to burden you with any extra chores."

"It's not that I'm not pleased," he said quickly. "But I had hoped we could begin saving for a move to Iowa. There's land for sale there, good land, and I've thought of writing to my brother Hiram, to ask him to come work with me. He's the best farmer I know."

"How could you ask us to move to Iowa?" Mary Elizabeth's voice quivered. "At least here we're a reasonable distance from Papa and Mama and Sarah and John."

Charles pulled at the ends of his moustache, then turned away. "There's nothing to fret over. It was just an idle notion," he said, hoping to sound as encouraging as possible.

He'd hoped his wife would not be quarrelsome about a move, that she had come to understand that Charles was simply not a schoolmaster. Apparently she hadn't noticed his growing discontent.

Of course, he wasn't much of a farmer or miner, either. If that were the case, what was he left with?

Eva Bowles was born after another long and exhausting birth. Peering at her red, swollen cheeks and furrowed brows, Charles shook his head; how would he manage with two daughters?

Mary Elizabeth was clearly disappointed. "Next time," she whispered.

"Don't," he said. She'd survived; that was all he cared about.

Everything else was unimportant. At least less important. He picked up his daughter and smiled. Who'd have ever thought he'd be a father.

He glanced back at Mary Elizabeth. "She's a fine baby," he said. "A fine baby, indeed. Come, take a look at her."

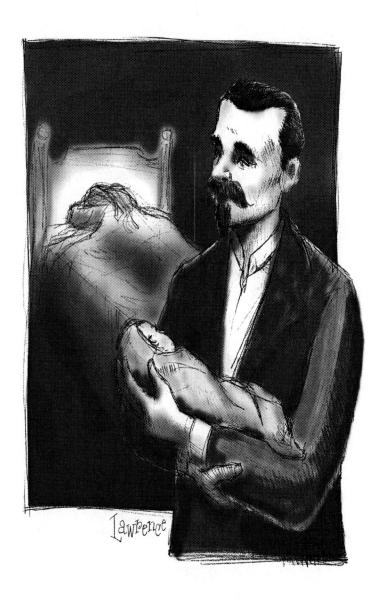

CHAPTER 18

As the spring and summer of 1860 waned, Charles knew his plan to move Mary Elizabeth and the girls to Iowa would have to be discarded. Summer storms had brought rain, more rain than anyone could remember for this time of year. Roads had been washed away and bridges and ferries had been destroyed by floods.

But Charles needed something to distract him. Mary Elizabeth had encouraged him to hire out for extra work, at least through the fall. Anything to get him out from underfoot.

He said he'd check with their neighbors.

One such neighbor, who quickly became a friend, was Lewis Disbrow. He and Charles talked of California and mining, and the old hunger to seek a fortune once more took hold in Charles' mind.

"A woman just doesn't understand a man's heart," said Charles to Lewis one cool but bright spring day in 1861. "She has no idea how much I hate teaching."

"I won't ever marry," returned Lewis.

Charles laughed. "Truth be told, marriage is hard to avoid. If only a man didn't feel so tied down after all is said and done."

"Well, your Mary Elizabeth is a fine woman and makes a mean meat pie. But that ain't enough. Besides, I'm gonna join up when war comes. With all these states seceding, it won't be long now, and I don't know that this new president's gonna be able to put a stop to it."

Charles picked up a pebble and threw it across the dusty lane that meandered past the house. "War does seem inevitable. But I shan't go. Mary Elizabeth's in the family way."

"Again? Well, you are the cock of the walk, aren't you, Charles?"

Charles frowned. It wasn't Mary Elizabeth's fault she was with child for a third time, he reminded himself sternly. But she didn't seem troubled by the notion; in fact, she seemed pleased. She had declared it would be a boy this time.

She didn't seem to understand that boy or girl, it wasn't another baby he yearned for.

Ironically, a letter from Hiram had also arrived. Slipping his hand into his coat pocket, Charles removed it. He'd told Lewis he'd read it to him.

His brother's affable greeting tugged at old affections. "Dearest Charles."

"Hiram's one of your younger brothers?"

"Younger but smarter," said Charles. He cleared his throat and continued, "You can't know what a delight it was to receive your letter, though it was dated more than three months ago. Mama has read it until the paper is nearly worn thin. She has forgiven you, brother. You must believe me."

Charles hesitated before going on. "We heard from Sarah that you took a wife and have two daughters and settled not far from her and John. That was good news to Mama who misses Sarah more than she admits."

Charles looked up. "Sarah and Mama fought like cats and dogs, but still, they were close."

He read on, "I, too, am married, to Ann, a woman of great character and wit. She is also with child, our first, due any day. To her credit, she never complains, but works alongside Mama as if nothing is amiss. I am a fortunate man.

I have thought long and hard of your plan to move to

Iowa. I am flattered you think me a good hand. And as much as I desire to please Papa, I have a mind to take you up on your offer, if you are still so decided. There is not enough here to keep us all without great sacrifice.

No doubt there is much controversy there about the possibility of war. I have heard that several states will secede if Mr. Lincoln is elected. I, for one, am tired of their ignoble attitudes and hope that war comes soon. Mama has become a staunch abolitionist, which is most surprising. Papa says very little but works hard..."

Charles glanced over at Lewis. "Mama's always been plainspoken, though she never bucked the old man."

Remembering Mother suddenly filled him with homesickness. The notion surprised him more than he'd have thought. But perhaps it was time he went home for a visit. Take Mary Elizabeth and the girls to meet their grandparents, uncles, and aunts.

He reread the date on the letter; it was more than five months old, and so much had happened in that time. Abe Lincoln had indeed been inaugurated. And, as Hiram had suggested, several states—Alabama, Florida, Georgia, Louisiana, Mississippi, Texas, and South Carolina—had seceded and formed the Confederate States of America.

And it wouldn't be long until the war came as well.

CHAPTER 19

A third daughter was born on June 6, but Mary Elizabeth refused to hold her. No amount of pleading could induce her to take the pale child into her arms.

Charles held the fragile infant while he paced back and forth across the narrow space separating bed and doorway. Mary Elizabeth would have to take the child soon. The midwife had left with the warning that she needed suckling, and, though Ida and Eva were waiting patiently in the front room, they would be wanting some attention soon.

Charles crossed to the bed. "Mary Elizabeth Bowles, this child needs you. She's beautiful. Look at her. It doesn't matter that she's not a boy."

Mary Elizabeth turned her face to the wall.

Charles frowned. "Please, have I been the sort of husband to make such demands? I am not my father, Mary Elizabeth. Now take her."

The child whimpered.

"I have nothing for her, do you hear me?" His temper, not easily flared, was rising. "I won't tolerate much more of this ridiculousness. Good grief, she doesn't even have a name."

Reluctantly, Mary Elizabeth took the child.

"She's a pretty little thing," he soothed. "Perhaps the prettiest of them all."

The baby suckled noisily at first. "She does have a lovely face," Mary Elizabeth whispered.

"And a name," Charles reminded her. "What sort of

name should we give her?"

"What do you prefer?"

Charles hesitated. He hadn't a fig of a notion, but such a declaration would likely bring Mary Elizabeth to tears all over again. He took a deep breath. "I once thought Lillian a good name."

"I like that," said Mary Elizabeth. "Lillian Bowles."

Charles stepped back and waited until Mary Elizabeth closed her eyes and relaxed, then he exited and pulled the door shut quietly behind him.

He sighed. His wife's pale complexion unnerved him. Obviously child-birthing was taking its toll, on not only her physical strength, but her emotional strength, as well.

He glanced over at Ida who was teaching Eva how to thread a needle. She looked up and smiled.

"Eva wants to know why Mama is too sick to get up. I told her that having a baby is hard work."

Charles agreed. "Yes, it is, perhaps the hardest work any woman has to do."

Eva pouted. "No baby."

Ida shook her curls and laughed. "Silly," she said in grown-up fashion. "That's what Mothers do."

Charles laughed in spite of himself. "Yes, I suppose. Now, who wants to help Papa with supper?"

Ida got to her feet and pulled Eva to hers. "Mama said we were to fix supper. Men don't cook. That's what she said."

Charles feigned disappointment. "So what do men do?"

Ida sighed impatiently. "You know what they do, Daddy. They work. But Mrs. Disbrow says that only good men work. Lazy men sit around talking about work."

CHAPTER 20

It was a bright August morning. Charles stood up and reached for his pocket watch.

"You might as well say it out loud," Mary Elizabeth said, putting her fork down.

Charles shoved the watch back into his vest pocket. "This isn't easy."

"Nothing is easy," said Mary Elizabeth. "Or, should I say, nothing has been easy for us." She raised her eyebrows as if daring him to disagree.

He knew he had to speak plainly. He'd been avoiding it for weeks. Lewis, who had reminded him once more that waiting would not make leaving easier to bear, had announced that he was enlisting, with or without Charles. "I'm not much of a school teacher."

"You're better than you think."

"I find it more and more frustrating and there's no money in it."

Mary Elizabeth shrugged. "That's true."

"I'd like to try farming, but we don't have the money to make a start."

Distracted by Lillian who had begun fussing in her cradle, Mary Elizabeth got up. Charles watched the two of them, Mother and Child.

Mary Elizabeth turned back to Charles. "You could do any number of things," she said crisply. "You are an intelligent man, Charles."

"That could be debated," he said, hoping to make light

his wife's remark.

"So, you're enlisting. To find something more interesting to do with your life."

The abruptness of Mary Elizabeth's declaration unnerved him. "A man can get ahead when the war is over, if he understands what's possible."

"What's possible?" snapped Mary. "What's possible is that you won't come home at all. Or that you'll come home without an arm or leg. How can you say a man can get ahead? What does that mean, Charles? More, what should it mean to me?"

Charles didn't have an answer.

Mary Elizabeth straightened her shoulders. He could see she was angrier than he'd ever seen her. "I'll see to it there's plenty of everything," he offered, wanting to stifle her bitterness. "I've already spoken to the Disbrows and they want you and the girls to stay on. I repaired the porch swing this morning," he added, as if that should make a difference.

Mary Elizabeth bit her lip. "It's not just money we need," she snapped.

"I know, but—" Charles said.

Mary Elizabeth waved a hand through the air. "Don't, Charles, don't try to explain. Or apologize—not now."

Charles heaved a sigh. "In truth, this could be an opportunity, for me, for us."

"An opportunity." Mary Elizabeth whispered the words, then shook her head.

"Aside from that, it's every man's duty. I know I've not said this well, but I do feel something for the cause, Mary Elizabeth. Even my mother's become an abolitionist."

Mary Elizabeth's terse response surprised him. "Yes, well, I've read too many lists of the dead or captured to feel something for the cause."

In September, 1862, at Fairview Park in Decatur,

Charles, Lewis Disbrow, and more than 900 other men, most from Macon County, were mustered into service by Captain Wainwright of the regular Union army. Each man pledged his allegiance, but the simple words were a solemn reminder of the seriousness of their duty.

The 116th Volunteer Illinois Infantry was to be commanded by Col. Nathan W. Tupper and Lt. Col. James P. Boyd, two men held in high regard by the citizens of Decatur and its neighboring communities. They were men to be trusted, thought Charles. They would be good leaders.

It was a warm, blustery day. Men and women from all over had gathered to observe the swearing in and to catch a glimpse of General Grant, who had come to Decatur from Memphis. Mary Elizabeth, her face hidden under a large, beribboned bonnet, stood under a shade tree with Lillian on one hip and Eva at her side. Ida sat on the grass at her feet, hands clasped together.

On the far side of the green, Charles stood shoulder to shoulder with Lewis, half-listening to the series of brief speeches being made by the assorted dignitaries. The day was intensely bright, and the clarity of the blue Illinois sky seemed to reflect the clarity of Charles' growing determination to make good his decision to go to war.

He scanned the row of faces and settled on General Grant, a small man with an unexceptional demeanor and somewhat shoddy appearance. Many had said that the man's rapid promotions were unwarranted, but Charles sensed that the outward appearance of a man did not always reflect his inner strength.

After a drum roll, the brief ceremony ended.

Ida, her straw hat in one hand, ran forward. "Papa! Did you like the parade?"

"Oh, yes," he said, bending down to sweep her up into his arms. "The drums and the guns were exciting, weren't they?"

"I want to be in the parade, too," she said.

"I think perhaps you have some growing up to do before you can do any marching. Besides, you're a young lady and ladies do not go off to war."

"Why not?" She tossed her long curls defiantly.

Charles and Lewis laughed but Mary Elizabeth, approaching them in long strides, frowned. "Don't be filling her head with grand notions about war," she said. "Ida, war is a terrible thing. Men die in war."

Ida looked down at her father. "Are you going to die, Papa?"

"Certainly not," returned Charles, glancing at his wife. "Your papa is very smart and can do things not every man can do."

"You can?" Ida said, her voice reflecting simple amazement.

"I promise," Charles said, carefully setting her on the ground.

Mary Elizabeth moved closer to Charles. "Do not," she whispered, "make promises that you cannot possibly keep. And until I see you walk back across our threshold, do not promise me that you can't be shot down. There are plenty of widows in this town whose husbands promised the same thing."

CHAPTER 21

Company B, along with several other newly-formed companies, was quartered at Camp Macon, not far from Decatur. Though not yet incorporated into the general war plan, the Illinois regiments were to become an important new element in Grant's scheme to move against the South.

The first weeks were filled with marching and waiting. Supplies were sparse, including ammunition and clothing, and most soldiers purchased what they needed from the sutlers. Occasionally, patrols were sent out into the countryside to scavenge for provisions, but some men simply stole what they felt they needed.

Not until the first week of November did the regiment receive orders to move.

"Where're we headed?" asked Private Patrick Burke. He fingered the butt of his musket as the irregular column of men tramped down the muddy road.

Col. Tupper and Lt. Col. Boyd were the only men on horseback, and, except for the wagoneers and sutlers trailing behind, everyone else was afoot.

"I hear we're movin' down to Memphis," said Lewis Disbrow. He had been promoted to sergeant after his father decided to purchase his commission. "We're joinin' Sherman's army."

"How'd you hear that?" quipped Burke. "I thought we were marchin' under McClernand."

"The sergeant's got ears," returned Private Henry Nesbitt with a smile. A tall, lean man, his features appeared

73

chiseled out of his oblong face. He carried his weapon across his broad shoulders, his bony arms wrapped around either end of his gun as if it were a yoke.

Young Cyrus Tolles and Martin Shelton joined the small party of men moving in pairs down the road.

"I wager we beat them rebs before the Year's up," said Cyrus, nodding his head in rhythm to his jocular step. "The war can't go on forever and we got more men than them."

"The rebs may be fools but they ain't all cowards," Burke said, and he frowned at the blonde-haired adolescent. "So don't be too cocksure of yourself, least ways not till after our first taste of fightin'. I hear it's nothin' for half a dozen men to run the other direction once the fightin' commences. An' we ain't licked 'em yet, have we?"

Cyrus snickered. "I'll shoot any louse that runs away myself."

Henry Nesbitt shook his head. "I've already lost two brothers in this war," he said. "And there's one more at home after me, but I made him promise to look after Ma. I'm telling you, these rebs got more grit than polish, so you all just keep your wits about you when they come at us."

"My cousin Jacob took a bullet at Winchester, in the Shenandoah," said Martin Shelton. "Mr. Stonewall Jackson surprised 'em that day. That's when I decided to enlist."

Nesbitt shuffled on. "Both my brothers died at Shiloh, in the first day of fighting. They never stood a chance. Grant just wasn't expectin' the attack. I think he figgered he couldn't be beat."

Charles, keeping step with Lewis, walked in silence. There was little to say as he listened to the men relate battles their brothers and neighbors had fought.

"Well, Sherman's crazy enough to lead us into purgatory," announced Cyrus.

Charles smiled. "I met Sherman a couple times," he said, "back in California. He was running a bank the last time I saw him."

"Maybe he'll have mercy on us then," whispered Shelton in exaggerated tones.

Everyone laughed.

But November merged into December and the Illinois recruits, now gathered in Memphis, waited for further instructions. The 15th Army Corps, including the 116th Illinois Infantry, was placed under the direct leadership of Division Commander Gen. Morgan Smith and Brigade Commander Gen. Giles Smith.

Charles, as restless as everyone else, spent much of his free time reading the small Bible Mary Elizabeth had given him. And, though he'd penned his wife and daughters a half-dozen letters, he hadn't mailed any. He knew Mary Elizabeth was still angry. Her first and only letter to him had been terse, revealing little except information about the weather and the girls.

He unfolded his own most recent attempt:

"My dearest Mary Elizabeth and children,

I received your November 15 letter yesterday. It was wonderful to hear from home, knowing that all is well. I was pleased to hear of the Disbrows' good harvest and their invitation to Thanksgiving supper. Lewis received letters from home stating that his parents were likewise glad to have you share the holiday with them. It must have been a grand feast.

The storm you mentioned sounded severe, but I am happy that Lewis's brother stopped by to repair the roof. Do not be afraid to spend what money you must. I have arranged to have my salary sent to you. Please let me know if something goes awry.

Rations here are sparse and though we have not yet gone into battle, I hear that we will be moving out soon. It is difficult to sit and wait, with only thoughts of home to warm us. As I promised, I have every intention of returning to you and the girls.

Before leaving Cairo, I bought a small silver cup for Lillian from one of the sutlers. Their prices are high, but I wanted to send something home for Christmas. There is also something for you and Ida and Eva—my four lovely women. I must trust the sutler's honesty and hope you receive the package soon. His wife assured me that she would take care of it herself as she has lost her only son to this war and will treat my gifts with special care.

There is little else to say. Please kiss the girls for their papa.

Charles."

He'd wanted to sign the letter with an affectionate salutation, but most likely, Mary Elizabeth would disdain any attempt to woo her.

He quickly refolded the letter and slipped it into the envelope Lewis had found for him. He would drop it off with the good sutler's wife.

CHAPTER 22

It was on the 13th of December that the 15th Army Corps received its orders. As to destination, no one seemed sure.

Morale among the veteran troops had dropped even more as defeat followed defeat; only the new recruits welcomed the call to battle. A few soldiers even talked of desertion, saying that it wouldn't be such a crime. After all, unless the Union managed to turn the tide in the next few weeks, the Confederates might just win the war.

"These old soldiers are nothin' but worn out and wasted," announced Cyrus Tolles. "I tell ya, we'll win this war and be finished with it!"

"I just keep prayin' that the Lord don't desert me when I have to fire this muzzle-loader for real," mumbled Patrick Burke. "Wish we had some of those Spencer rifles we keep hearin' so much about."

Lewis agreed. "You'd think if they were gonna send us into this mess they'd give us the best weapons they could muster."

"Wish you was right," Burke said. "With McClernand and Sherman at the lead, we'll be in the thick of the fight afore long. Maybe they're just thinkin' that it'd be a waste to give us better weapons."

On the morning of the 19th, the 116th found itself boarding The Planet, a moderately-sized vessel and, amidst a cacophony of horns, whistles, and cheering, the fleet of steamships loaded with Union troops headed down the

Mississippi River.

Pungent odors from the inky trails of smoke, coupled with the stench of dirty men, quickly settled over the vessel like a wet, woolen blanket. Crowded together, men leaned against the railings and each other, waiting for news of their destination. Numbering 30,000 men, it was clear that the upcoming campaign must be an important one.

Cyrus and Martin, jovial and animated, couldn't wait for action, while Charles, Patrick Burke, and Henry Nesbitt, each aloof and pensive, turned their attention to the shoreline. Lewis had found a corner in the stern where he could nap.

Scattered and half-hidden by trees and brush, the nearly-abandoned plantations stood like sentinels. Charles was fascinated by the deep greens and grays that colored the landscape and by the heady aromas that seemed to hang in the air like the strands of moss hanging from the trees like ribbons.

Occasionally the troopers called out to tattered slaves watching from the shoreline. A few children ran down to the marshy beaches, waving and calling out in languages Charles could not understand.

"They're a sight, aren't they?" Henry remarked. "Wonder what they think of this action?"

"No doubt they're watching and waiting," said Charles. "Who can say what will happen to them eventually."

Henry nodded. "The world isn't gonna be a friendly place for the likes of them, whether we prevail or not. The poor fools can't do anything but cow-tow to a master. Think they can even think on their own?"

Charles thought of his old friend Jim Beckwourth. Colored didn't seem to affect him. "I'd wager that under the right circumstances a man, colored or not, can think clearly enough."

"Maybe so," Henry said. He shoved a sliver of a stick between his front teeth. "I'd like to think my brothers died for something more than a few big words."

"The Union is more than just a word," returned Charles.

After a long pause, Henry asked, "You think we'll see trouble soon?"

Charles nodded. "Sherman looks grim. I got a peek at him this morning."

"But you haven't spoken to him yet?"

"No."

Henry rolled the stick around on his tongue. "Well, I got this itch, right between my shoulders, and it's got me thinking. It won't be long before we meet Johnny Reb."

It was no secret that the rebels controlled the river from Vicksburg to Baton Rouge and that the Mississippi represented the heart of the South. The Federals would have to capture it if they hoped to stop Lee and his troops from advancing.

It was also no secret that the Union needed a victory before it fell prey to greater fear and disillusionment. Disgruntled Northerners wanted a victory soon. Others feared that Lincoln's plan to sign an Emancipation Proclamation would alienate, even destroy the possibility of reconciling the South to the North, that is, if the North prevailed.

In truth, Charles wasn't sure what Mr. Lincoln could do to insure the outcome of the war. He even doubted that the good Lord himself could alter the course the war seemed destined to take.

CHAPTER 23

"It don't feel like Christmas," Cyrus mumbled. He replaced the cap on Martin's flask and handed it to Lewis who took two hearty gulps.

"Sure don't," returned Martin bitterly. "'Cept for the cold."

"You think we'll ever get out of these swamps?" piped Patrick.

Though Federal gunboats had secured a length of the Yazoo River, the Confederates still held Vicksburg, which meant that a Yankee assault would come soon.

The men moved on, slogging through the marsh that surrounded the remains of a plantation house. With their weapons cradled in their arms and their knapsacks strapped to their backs, they were unable to move quickly.

"Like I said, it don't feel like Christmas at all," Cyrus said.

"Christmas or no," returned Patrick, "I got an ache the size of the Missouri runnin' through my guts. When do we eat?"

"When we get to dry land," said Charles. Until now he'd remained outside the conversation. Like children, they could hardly walk without talking, and he often found it irritating.

Henry Nesbitt hushed the younger men. "You fools gotta learn to keep your mouths shut. Do you wanna wake up the Johnnies before it's time? Besides, there's nothin' to be gained by thinkin' 'bout food or holidays. We all know it's Christmas and there ain't nothin' we're gonna celebrate tonight."

Henry broke in, "Well, just so's long as we don't have to spend next Christmas sloggin' through this mud, that's all that I care about."

"That's a soberin' thought," snapped Patrick. "You think it's likely, Charles?"

"No," said Charles, wishing everyone would shut up.

Their first skirmish took place on December 27th. Under a hail of shot, shell, and shrapnel, the Federals, sent to attack the Vicksburg fortifications in a frontal assault, ran like quail. The only hiding places they found were in the murky shallows of Chickasaw Bayou, and even the new recruits realized that every waterway surrounding Vicksburg had been fortified. The Confederates had prepared for a major battle.

After the first failed assault, Charles and Henry found themselves together, caught between the impenetrable Confederate defense and fragments of the ravaged Federal brigade. On their bellies in the mud and bog, the two kept their heads buried in the crooks of their arms as they waited for a lull in the shelling.

"I ain't seen Cyrus or Martin or Lewis or Patrick," whispered Henry.

Charles flinched as a hail of mud and stones fell like rain from the smoke-filled sky.

Henry squirmed closer. "We're like sittin' ducks, Charles. I don't think we can move forward or back."

Charles nodded. Their only protection was to stay where they were, yet how could they survive if they didn't move out of harm's way? He rolled his face toward Henry, all but his eyes hidden by his tattered, mud-stained sleeve. "We'll wait 'til dark."

"They had to see us comin', don't you think?"

"We were in their sights plain enough." Charles' throat

burned from the acrid smoke and he was thirsty. "Can you reach my canteen?"

Henry grabbed Charles' knapsack, which had fallen off to his left, but several minie balls passed overhead and a man just a stone's throw away shrieked. "Damn, that was close," said Henry. He dragged Charles' canteen forward. "There's gotta be a better way of gettin' up to those bluffs than on our bellies."

Certainly there had to be a better way to attack the rebs, thought Charles. The cost was already staggering, the dead strewn like rag dolls along the shoreline or floating, half-submerged, their arms moving eerily over the surface of the water. Men, alive but too wounded to run, sat and wept, aware that the end was inevitable. The rest hunkered down, like Henry and Charles, waiting for the gunfire to resume.

In the next instant, the earth shuddered and Charles buried his head in his arms. Black, pungent smoke, like a heavy shroud, swept over him.

"Tarnation! I took a ball, Charles—"

Charles swung his head around, but could not distinguish the outline of his friend in the black cloud. "Where?"

Henry moaned. "Shoulder."

"Let me see."

Henry tried to chuckle. "Think you can see anything in this soup?"

"Let me see," Charles repeated.

"It's surely a long way to my heart. Leave it be for now."

Again the ground trembled as rapid-fire explosions were followed by shrieks of men being hit and killed. A shredded blue cap landed in the dirt only inches from them.

Charles knocked it out of the way.

"Oh, Lord," Henry whispered, "have mercy upon us."

CHAPTER 24

The battle had been a disastrous mistake, and it didn't take long before word spread: Sherman had miscalculated the strength of the enemy and General Van Dorn's advancing Confederates had slowed reinforcements. More men than anyone could tally had been gunned down, while not a strip of enemy territory had been taken.

Henry was in the hospital. The minie ball had lodged deep, and there wasn't much the surgeon could do. He'd given the semi-conscious Henry some morphine, but that didn't mean much, thought Charles, as he moved down the row of tents to his own.

It wasn't long before orders to march again came through. All able-bodied troops would be leaving the Yazoo to move up to the Arkansas River, 120 miles northwest of Vicksburg.

"Well, Henry," said Charles when he and Lewis went to visit him a day later, "looks like you'll be spared this fight."

"I may not look like I can carry a weapon," Henry said, placing his feet on the ground, "but I already got permission to rejoin the outfit."

"Henry, I don't think—" Charles began.

"Too late. Orders is orders and I'm goin'."

Gathering up his gear early the next morning, Henry announced, "My legs still work and I can fire a rifle one-handed if needs be."

Lewis frowned. "You won't be worth as much as a 3-legged hound."

Henry glared at Lewis before turning to Charles. "I guess a man oughta be able to choose his own dyin' place."

The attack on the Arkansas Post was the company's first taste of victory. Held by only a few thousand Confederates, the entire garrison, including 46,000 rounds of ammunition, was captured. In spite of the victory, however, Company B had sustained major losses in the two-day campaign, coming out of the battle with only twenty-five survivors.

Sergeant Christian Riebsame was promoted after Lieutenant John Taylor was killed, and those lost included several of Charles' acquaintances from Decatur, including Reuben Bills and Abraham Shepherd.

Sitting around the campfire two days later, Lewis prattled on about the fortunate turn of events. "I knew soldierin' could be a sight better than what we saw at Vicksburg."

Patrick glanced over at Charles. "You think he'll make captain someday?"

"Sho' 'nough," drawled Charles in exaggerated fashion. Raising his tin cup, he added, "You fought splendidly, Sergeant, to be sure."

"I did, didn't I?" nodded Lewis. "I killed no less than a dozen rebels, even before you fellows caught up to me."

"Lordy, but you are a wonder," Henry whispered.

Charles took a hard look at Henry. Disheveled and wan, the man was still suffering. He shuffled when he marched and had to sit down frequently to catch his breath. When no one was watching, he held his shoulder and took slow deep breaths.

Impatient with the men as they recounted the Union's success, Charles got up and crossed over to his bed. He needed some space and quiet.

He also needed to write Mary Elizabeth and the girls.

He owed her more than a letter, though. He owed her an apology.

She had been right about the war, and he'd refused to listen, believing that the war could advance his opportunities in life. Clearly, just making it out alive would be his greatest achievement. He picked up his pencil and started to write.

Martin interrupted him. "You think Cyrus deserted, Charles?"

Up until now no one dared to ask the question because no one had seen the young soldier since the Vicksburg assault, and Cyrus Tolles's name had not been posted on any of the lists of dead or wounded.

Charles gathered his thoughts. "I don't know."

"Henry says men do funny things when they think they're gonna die. You think that's true?"

"I'm sure that any one of us might be surprised by what we choose in the face of death."

It was on January 27, two days before Grant was to arrive at Milliken's Bend that Henry Nesbitt collapsed with fever. Waking in the night, Charles heard Henry cry out, his voice a thin whisper. Clambering out of bed, Charles woke Lewis and the two of them helped Henry to the hospital tent. Dr. Barnes, his face unshaven and his eyes bloodshot from too little sleep, ushered them in.

He frowned and shrugged. "Find him a bed. I can't promise more than a look-see, though. We've got more sickness than we can tend to and there don't seem to be any reinforcements coming, at least not in the way of surgeons or nurses."

Henry slumped down on one of the few empty cots, grumbling, "All I need is a good night's sleep. There ain't nothing more than that to fret over."

"Well, then, get a good night's rest," returned Charles.

Lewis and Charles walked back to their camp in silence. The wind, having come up unexpectedly, whistled eerily, as if crying out from the darkness. It sent a chill down Charles' spine.

"In truth, he don't look good, Charles," said Lewis.

"He just needs rest."

"Yeah, and Cyrus ain't a coward," mumbled Lewis.

"Hush up, Lewis," snapped Charles.

CHAPTER 25

All the next day the rain came down in sweeping torrents. Assigned to one of the engineering projects General Grant had commissioned, Charles, Martin, Lewis, and Patrick worked alongside several hundred men, digging and shoveling mud.

"Grant ain't even here to give the orders," complained one trooper. "Why don't he slop around if he wants to dig a hole? Seems like we're goin' nowhere, just deeper into the mud."

"What kind of soldierin' is this anyhow?" grumbled another. "I'll take marchin' and shootin' over mud and rain."

"They say we're gonna cut a channel that'll dry up Vicksburg," said Lewis.   "You mean move the entire Mississippi?" crowed a third soldier. "That'll be a sight to see."

That night, after a quick, cold supper, Charles rushed through the rain-soaked camp to the field hospital.

He entered the tent cautiously, searching for Henry's familiar face, but all he spotted was an attendant stripping an empty cot.

"Can you tell me where Private Nesbitt is?"

"I'm sorry," the trooper said. "This here was his bed but he died more'n an hour ago." He turned and lumbered down the row of beds where other men lay, hollow-eyed, bloody, or grim.

Charles raced after him. "Hey, I'm looking for Private Henry Nesbitt."

The attendant stopped and turned back. "I told you. He's dead."

Charles took a careful, steadying breath. "No, you must have that wrong."

The soldier hesitated, then rubbed a hand across his bearded chin. "You a friend?"

"Yes. A friend," said Charles slowly.

"Well, then, maybe you could see that his personals get sent back home. I got 'em over here in a sack."

Numbly, Charles followed the attendant. There were only a few meager possessions, including a knife and small pocket watch Charles had never noticed before.

He tucked the items into his coat before stepping back out into the rain. He didn't even know to whom he should send them.

As he tramped on, he suddenly grew angry. Henry had been too good to die. Just like David.

CHAPTER 26

In March, the river began to recede and the roads dried out. General Grant, disappointed that his monumental canal scheme failed to matriculate, decided to keep a portion of his troops at Milliken's Bend, Young's Point, and Lake Providence. The rest of the troops he moved south, bypassing Vicksburg.

Sherman and the Fifteenth Army Corps, including Company B and the Eighth Missouri, marched up Black Bayou and Deer Creek in an attempt to protect Admiral Porter's gunboats. Even Sherman marched in, on foot.

Unexpectedly, a shower of musketry rained down on the ranks of exhausted soldiers. Dozens, even those in charge of the wheeled guns, had to run for cover.

"Charles!" Lewis cried. He had grabbed Charles by the sleeve and was yanking him into a ditch.

Charles shook him off. "I think Patrick's been hit."

"You can't sneak out there. You gotta wait."

Charles dropped his chin to the embankment, nostrils burning from the choking smoke. He listened to the wails of the wounded, watched them writhe in the narrow road.

It was Chickasaw Bayou all over again.

"Look, they're running," said Lewis, pointing to the dozens of Federals who had suddenly begun to retreat into the brush and wood.

As soon as Charles and Lewis saw their opportunity, they, too, slipped back. When they reached a ragged group of men in a clearing, they recognized several from their outfit.

"The day's not over yet," Lieutenant Riebsame was saying to the wide-eyed soldiers clumped around him, "and this is not a retreat. The general ordered us to keep moving, no matter what the cost." His eyes narrowed as he scanned the men's faces. "We've got to find those rebel batteries. Admiral Porter's fleet is waiting for us and we cannot let them be taken by surprise."

Lewis jumped forward. "Sir, I've got an idea as to its whereabouts. I spotted where the ball of fire was comin' from."

Riebsame raised his brows questioningly. "Okay, Sergeant. Take Smoot and Rutherford. But be sure and send us word when you've succeeded. We'll be coming up behind you."

"Yes, sir!" snapped Lewis.

"Let me go as well, sir," said Charles.

"Certainly, Bowles," returned the lieutenant.

Falling into step beside Lewis, Charles whispered, "Next time you want to volunteer, let me know ahead of time."

"Hey, you didn't have to come."

"Yeah, well, I can't let you go wandering off by yourself."

Lewis chuckled. "Come on, maybe we'll find Patrick and Martin."

The four men moved carefully through the undergrowth. Lewis, who seemed more hound than man, took the lead, directing every step through the curtain of dense foliage. Finally, as the sun slipped behind the tops of the trees, he raised his hand.

The faint whisper of his own breath was all that Charles heard as he drew up beside Lewis, that and the distant musket fire and frequent booms shaking the earth under his feet.

Lewis raised a finger to his lips, eyes straining to catch

sight of anything unfamiliar in the heavy growth beyond them. "On the ridge. Do you hear it? It's a cannon and it's been dug into the hillside. We're gonna have to take it."

Smoot, inching forward, whistled softly. "How do you figure we get close to it?"

"On our bellies, if we have to," returned Lewis.

Charles nodded. Lewis was right. Someone had to take out the big gun, or else the remaining soldiers and the ones coming after them would be nothing but chaff. "Lewis, we're right beside you."

They crawled along the darkened earth, getting to their knees only when they had to wrestle over a limb or through a stretch of prickly brush. Finally, they heard and felt the heat of the big gun. Lewis raised his hand above the rim of his cap.

With heart thumping and palms wet with anticipation, Charles positioned himself and his rifle. Smoot and Rutherford did the same.

When Lewis's order came, it was soft but clear. "Forward." Then he pushed himself onto his feet and began darting to the left and right.

Charles stayed at his heels and Smoot and Rutherford were not far behind. But it was Lewis who circled the gunners, hollering at the top of his lungs. Surprising the rebels, he fired point-blank. Charles fired second, then Smoot and Rutherford's carbines exploded in rapid succession.

When the smoke cleared, Lewis lay atop two Johnnies, body shaking, left arm quivering as blood ran down his sleeve.

Charles rushed forward and gathered him up in his arms.

"Agh! Careful," moaned Lewis.

Rutherford slipped an arm around Lewis's middle and helped Charles negotiate their retreat. Smoot picked up the spent carbines.

"We did it," murmured Lewis. He tried to focus on Charles but was quickly losing consciousness. "We got 'em, Charles."

Smoot's voice came to them from behind. "So what? We got one cannon. There are plenty more up ahead, half-buried and well fortified."

"Shut up," said Charles. "And keep moving."

Lewis did not regain consciousness but miraculously hung onto life. Shot in three places, no one could imagine how he had survived at all. Charles stayed beside him, until he heard that Patrick Burke had been killed in the first assault. When soldiers found his mutilated body, a letter stuffed into a pocket was used to identify his remains.

It was all Charles could do to visit the fresh mound of earth. After losing Henry, and with Lewis hardly alive, Patrick's death was like vinegar on an open wound.

Lewis died on April 15, seven days after Patrick.

It was Reibsame who gave Charles the news. Scratching the back of his head, the lieutenant sighed. "I'd rather be a soldier than a priest in this war."

Unable to speak, Charles stumbled away. When Martin found him early the next morning, he was still too drunk to stand.

"Come on, Sergeant, the lieutenant wants you. You gotta get back on your feet."

"Yeah?"

"Yeah. This is enough."

No, thought Charles, it wasn't. On the other hand, no amount of booze would ease the pain. He pushed Martin away and stood up. "Get outa my way."

Charles was given a promotion for valor.

CHAPTER 27

A bell clanged as smoke billowed out above the transport. Even with clouds hovering overhead, it wafted gray and thick, the smell oily and heavy. In the pale morning light, the river was gray, too.

Charles shivered. They were on the move again.

The transport was crowded as men pushed for a better position near the railing. Charles let the troopers pass; he was content to sit near the smokestacks where, at least, he could keep comparatively warm. The crisp morning air cut through the fabric of his coat as raindrops landed on his shoulders. The storm was fast approaching.

Martin squeezed in beside Charles. "When will we get to where we're goin'?"

Charles shrugged. "There's supposed to be a mountain of felled trees somewhere ahead. I heard the lieutenant say that Wheeler's Cavalry was burning bridges and leaving trees in their wake, just to slow us down."

"Why don't the rebs just give up? Cain't they see the end is comin'?"

Charles took a deep breath. He had to appreciate the tenacity of the Confederates even if he despised their mission. "They aren't going to die peaceably. Would you?"

Martin chewed on the end of a cigar. "We better find a place to roost soon," he grumbled, ignoring Charles' question. "I gotta take a piss before it leaks outa my ears."

Charles smiled. "If you can't find a place along the railing, there's a bucket at the other end of the deck."

When the fleet of transports finally docked, the men were herded out. With hardly an hour's rest, they were marching. Rumor had it that they were to hold the river bridge at Beaufort while the enemy held fast at Kalketatchie. In order to do so, the soldiers had to cross a swamp nearly three miles wide.

Charles and Martin, along with a dozen other men, climbed aboard one of the many pontoon floats being slipped into the water. Easing along the swamp's grassy edge, they were not far from the enemy line.

Martin's voice was a hoarse whisper. "I think we got the upper hand this time."

Charles held his breath. He wasn't too all-fire sure about anything. He'd learned that the rebels were masters at being where they weren't supposed to be.

When he realized that the men on the rafts ahead had slipped into the marsh water, he whistled softly. He motioned to his men, then slid into the murky depths until his feet found the soft, spongy swamp bottom. Clutching his rifle above his head, he steadied himself before sloshing on. Darkness was descending quickly, so Charles kept his eyes on the faint shadow men in the distance.

Without warning, a battery of gunshot splattered across the surface of the water. Everyone froze.

Charles glanced back at the startled, horrified young soldiers behind him. "Keep moving!" He waved them on with the butt of his gun. "Our cannon will be the next guns you hear."

Plunging deeper into the water, he held his breath. It was cold, but it wasn't the cold water that made him shiver. Gunshots danced around him like marbles and the men were crying out, some hit, others just terrified.

When Charles reached the shoreline, he scrambled up, water running out of his boots and pants. "Let's get to that rise," he whispered to the men surrounding him. They hunkered over more like a passel of newborn chicks than a

94

contingent of soldiers.

As they topped the narrow ridge, Charles scanned the surrounding landscape. Below them lay the city of Columbia, dark and crowded; a short distance away, he spotted enemy targets, but they were retreating into the curtain of night. He signaled to his men to don their bayonets.

Martin was the first to comply, and jumping up, he cried, "We got 'em on the run, boys! After me!"

Charles' heart thumped as the same craziness took root. "Come on," he hissed to those still crouched and shaking. The weight of the gun drew him forward, and the heat of the bullets whizzing past made him angry.

"Let's go!"

In the next flash, he spotted the ghostly image of— who? Lewis? Yes, there—no, there—ahead of him, skirting the enemy's bullets, dancing through the brush as if he was enjoying himself. The fool turned and waved him forward, a smile across his homely face. And Henry and Patrick were close behind.

But before Charles could catch up to them, they had vanished.

Shaken and angry, he cursed. "Damn you all anyway."

Then he remembered that two dozen young, foolish soldiers were following him now.

He glanced back, then steeled himself. He couldn't make a mistake, and he wouldn't let them die.

"Come on, men! It's time to finish this war."

CHAPTER 28

"Boss, you need some help wit' that?"

Charles turned to shake his head, then stopped and shrugged. He'd seen the hordes of freed blacks tramping along behind the troops but hadn't had occasion to converse with any of them. Some of the soldiers taunted them or treated them as poorly as Charles imagined the Confederates did. "Actually, I could use some help."

The black youth nodded, eyebrows raised. "Yes, sir," he said. Hoisting the trunk onto his shoulder with hardly a grunt, he took a step forward. "Where to, Boss?"

"The supply tent. This way. Steady now. That trunk is full and the captain wouldn't want it to break apart."

"Yes, sir."

The two skirted the rows of camp tents where soldiers reclined, some sitting around small fires, sipping coffee, others standing in groups, talking and joking.

There was little else to do at the end of a day.

Finding a niche where the trunk would fit, Charles directed the young man to lower it carefully.

"It weren't so heavy," he said.

Charles smiled. "Perhaps not, but I appreciate the good turn. Here, for your trouble," he added, pulling out a two-cent piece and some hardtack.

"Thank ye." The boy shoved the coin into his pocket, the hardtack between his teeth.

Charles studied his profile. Well-muscled and standing nearly six feet, the boy couldn't be more than fifteen.

Without knowing why, he said, "Are you hungry?"

"Always hungry. But they feeds us good here."

"Well, follow me. We've got some coffee and biscuits. You like coffee?"

"Yes, sir."

Martin and Hank sat up when Charles and the boy entered camp. Felix, harmonica in hand, froze.

"Who's he?" Martin asked.

Charles turned. "You got a name?"

"Yes, sir. Called Castor, Boss."

"Castor?" Charles smiled. "Do you know who Castor was?"

"No, Boss."

Charles laughed. "Tell me, do you like horses?"

"Yes, sir, Boss. I takes good care of the horses. Dey love me."

"No doubt," smiled Charles. He reached for the coffee-pot and poured a half-cup for Castor and another for himself.

Felix stared at Castor. "Sergeant, I really don't know as I want some darkie here drinkin' our coffee. Why don't he go back to where the others are? They got their own kind."

Hank grumbled his agreement.

Charles straightened his shoulders, his smile gone. "Private, I think it'd be best if you took yourself off someplace, somewhere out of my sight. And take Hank with you. Then, when you're feeling less inclined to debate who and who isn't going to drink coffee by this fire, my fire, you can return. Meanwhile, Castor, take a seat."

Castor, at a loss for words, hesitated. "Don't want no trouble, Boss."

"Take a seat, Castor," Charles repeated, his eyes on Felix.

Martin, his expression dour, watched without a word. After Hank and Felix moved off, he whistled sharply.

"Charles, I'm afraid you may be creatin' enemies here."

"Stupidity and arrogance are two of man's greatest enemies," snapped Charles. He turned to Castor. "I do believe we have a tin of canned milk around somewhere, don't we, Martin? Why don't you open it up? I bet Castor's never had milk in his coffee."

"No, Boss, ain't never had. But no mind."

Martin, frowning, dug through his knapsack. "This here's the last can."

"All the better," Charles said.

"What's gotten into you?" whispered Martin, eyes narrowed.

"That's a good question. Wish I knew the answer," said Charles.

Martin shook his head. "This could lead to real trouble."

Charles ignored Martin's declaration as he cut a hole in the top of the tin with his pocketknife. Smiling, he poured a liberal dose of milk into Castor's cup.

"Boss," said Castor, holding up his left hand, "that's a heap of milk. Better save some for yerself."

"Don't like the stuff," Charles said.

Martin's voice cracked. "Damn, Charles, don't you see the men watchin' us?"

Charles didn't look up, but when he did, he was smiling.

It just didn't matter, he wanted to say. With all the craziness happening around them, he simply wanted to do something that felt good. Right now, that meant watching Castor smile as he enjoyed canned milk for the first time.

Martin's sigh was long and deep. "It's been a hard winter, Charles, I know. But there's no sense makin' enemies inside the camp as well as outside."

"You know what, Martin?" Charles nodded toward the

ex-slave. "Castor here is celebrating his new-found freedom. What a thing to think on, eh, Castor?"

"Reckon so, Boss."

Martin kicked at the tin cups scattered on the ground. "I'll keep my own counsel on that one."

"Fair enough," returned Charles blandly. He didn't harbor any ill will toward Martin. The boy had always been faithful and eager to please.

By evening, word of Charles' odd behavior had spread through camp, leaving in its wake heated discussions as to what should be done about the blacks who were accompanying Sherman's army as it crossed Georgia.

Defenders pointed out that the South had no intention of allowing blacks to roam freely, that their only protection was with the northern armies. Opponents felt that allowing ex-slaves to join the ranks of white soldiers endangered everyone, particularly the white soldiers if the ex-slaves were caught alongside them in a defeat.

Charles avoided all discussion of his behavior. For whatever reason, the satisfaction he felt in having done exactly what he wanted overruled any sense that he'd crossed some random line of decency.

"I'll be danged if I have to appease fools and idiots," he said to Martin later that evening. "Good grief, it was a cup of coffee."

And a lousy cup of coffee, to be sure.

CHAPTER 29

Though a warm day, the humidity tormented the sick and wounded, making them restless and irritable. One trooper, missing an arm and leaning heavily against a makeshift crutch, spat as Charles limped past him.

"They's never gonna let me go," he hissed. "Only got one eye worth a damn and can't see but double through it. I suppose you're outa here?"

Charles understood the man's bitterness. The field hospital was more of a morgue than a place of healing. He shrugged. "Any day now, though I've still got a hitch in my git-along."

The man grunted. Anyone's good fortune was but more of his bad luck.

Charles forced himself to keep walking. He had to get past the hospital tents, away from the sickness and death and the tirades and quarrels that went on all day.

Besides, in contrast to most of the men's injuries, his was not serious.

He wandered down to where a small creek tumbled over rocks, where clusters of elm trees lined the muddy bank, their limbs stretched out over the water like old women's arms. At least it was cooler in the shade, even if the flies were merciless. He slapped at several buzzing around his ears and sat down.

Rolling onto his left hip, he dipped his hands into the tepid water. Startled, a small snake slithered out from under a rock and into the undergrowth.

Charles sat back. If only he could escape as gingerly as

the snake.

Well, no matter. When the war was over, he would build on what was left of his life. With the war behind him, he'd put Mary Elizabeth and the girls first. It was about time.

He returned to the hospital tent and his cot, determined to make things right with Mary Elizabeth.

He had not written for far too long. Pulling out a square of stained paper and a pencil, he scratched the date.

"June 8, 1864"

"My dear Wife,

This has been the hardest of times. I know I have not written for two months or more, but I do so now, diligently. We crossed the Tennessee and entered Georgia weeks ago. All went well until we reached Resaca, Georgia. The battle lasted five days. It is too hard to tell you of all the good men we lost. Most of Company B is gone while others in the Illinois Volunteers were either seriously wounded or taken prisoner.

After Resaca, we advanced on Dallas and again, the fighting was hard. The sun beat down, though evenings were cool, and each morning we woke to a barrage of heavy artillery. Even now I hear the thundering inside my head.

By mid-May we had fashioned a line along the Pumpkin Vine creek. I cannot tell you of the balls that whistled past our ears, yet Martin and I held fast. When we reached New Hope Church and Allatoon, the horrible heat caused many to drop without a shot fired. We pushed so many rebs up the Kennesaw Mountain that they held the high ground and kept us pinned below.

The Kennesaws are three separate peaks, but they offered the Confederates extended cover. Dearest wife, long will I remember the Kennesaw, its high range covered with chestnut trees. Behind these hills sits the door to Atlanta, but each day the fighting grew heavier. Unfortunately, the enemy was entrenched when Sherman finally ordered an assault at two points south of the Kennesaw. The attack failed.

And, now I must confess that I was wounded. But do not fret. Though I took two balls, one only grazed me and one left me more aggravated than hurt. I am out of action only for the present, but am anxious to return to my men. Idleness is often worse than confronting the enemy, and battlefront hospitals are not for the living, in spite of the doctors' attempts to heal. But I will come home a whole man.

I wish I could write of something more pleasant, but the heat depletes me of my strength. I think of the garden you must be tending. Do the girls help you? No doubt they are as pretty as daisies. Give them a hug for their papa.

Your loving husband,

Charles."

CHAPTER 30

With the New Year came renewed determination to end the war. An exasperated Sherman announced that his army would march north, into South Carolina, the state considered by many to have started the war.

"We're gonna finish it off where it all began," the men repeated to each other.

Charles, once more assigned to scavenge for provisions, was directed to leave nothing behind for the rebels, nothing that might encourage or sustain them. Having been given the area to the west to survey, Charles decided to take fewer men with him. He knew there was a chance of violence, especially now that the Confederate army was desperate. No telling who might be hiding out.

Taking Martin, Felix, Hank and Jimmy, Charles' small band set out on foot. Trailing behind, with a pushcart, was Castor. The boy had refused to leave Charles, sleeping just outside his tent each night while following him around each day, responding when spoken to, but otherwise just watching and waiting.

Charles' camp mates had remained stonily silent, but he knew that he had created a situation that might not resolve itself easily.

No matter. Nothing had come down from the top brass and, since he was in charge of this detail, his decisions would stand without argument.

Or so he hoped.

Charles led his party through the timber, across a stream and down a narrow lane. Spotting a ramshackle barn, he whispered, "Felix, Jimmy! You circle to the right. Hank and Martin, around to the left. I'll come up from behind. Keep your eyes open."

The men slipped through the brush carefully, but the barnyard was deserted, and the only thing inside the barn was a broken down mule.

Laughing out loud, Felix cried, "Shall we shoot it?" He drew his rifle to his shoulder. "It's lame."

Charles hesitated. He didn't relish killing off an old mule.

"Sergeant?" Martin asked stiffly.

Charles took a slow, deep breath. He knew he wasn't supposed to leave anything that could be used by a Confederate, but good grief, who would want the worthless animal anyway?

"Oh, Boss," said Castor suddenly. "You don't want to shoot no mule. Tired as he is, I don't think he could pull a chicken, even if he had a mind to."

Felix grumbled, obviously disappointed that Charles couldn't make up his mind. "Sergeant, Captain's orders were clear."

"And you take orders from me, Private," Charles snapped. "Castor, take that mule and tie him to your cart. If you can keep him moving, he's yours."

Felix dropped his rifle, a frown replacing his look of astonishment. "It's a mistake," he grumbled.

Jimmy, who had remained quiet, followed Castor over to where the pathetic creature stood, its head nearly to the ground, ribs pressed against flesh, tail and mane mere wisps of hair. Jimmy nudged it while Castor coaxed it.

"Ah, Boss, I shorely will keeps him movin', yessir."

The mule, a motley shade of gray, wobbled a few steps and then stopped, but Castor, speaking softly and urgently, got the animal to move again.

Felix, as surly as he'd been the night he'd declared no

darkie should drink from his coffee pot, kept his narrowed gaze on Castor.

Charles knew the young trooper was angry, but he refused to give him the time of day. After all, Castor was as loyal and hardworking as any soldier he'd seen. And it seemed a useless act to put down a mule that the ex-slave might actually be able to doctor back to health. Hadn't the boy been named for one of Zeus's sons, a young man endowed with great courage and gifts?

CHAPTER 31

The rumor that rebel deserters would soon outnumber Lee's forces reinvigorated Sherman's army. It'd been reported many were starving, some had no weapons or ammunition, and even fewer owned shoes or coats. However, Charles had come to respect the grit these men possessed and cautioned his own men not to place too much stock in gossip. Even still, the men clung to the hope that the rebs were as anxious for the war to end as the Yankees.

"We got 'em by the heels," Martin declared as he and Jimmy joined Charles around the fire one March evening. They'd just returned from picket duty and were hungry and wet.

Jimmy held his open palms out over the flames. "Indeed, it must be true. Even Castor's a hero. Did you hear what he did, sergeant?"

Charles looked up, shook his head. He'd been busy all day sorting supplies, and the fact that the company was low on food, medicine, and supplies, weighed heavily on him.

"Well, that boy managed to capture a rebel all by himself," chuckled Martin. "Spotted the fool hidin' in a ditch, and before he knew what was what, this grayback raised up and pleaded with poor ole Castor to save him. Save *him*!"

Charles laughed. What sweet revenge, he thought.

Indeed, the event signaled a change for Castor as he suddenly took on a certain prominence, in spite of Felix or Hank's disdain. His reputation for doctoring animals had brought him fame throughout the camp; even the lieutenant had asked him to look over a few of the company's horses.

"It was a sight," said Jimmy. "And ought to make some fur fly!"

Felix, dragging into camp, dropped to the ground. He frowned at the young soldier's smiling face. "Any of you fellas seen Hank?"

Jimmy and Martin shook their heads.

"Not since early this mornin'," said Martin.

"Damn, he was right behind me comin' into camp," said Felix, shaking his head. "Then he was gone. There weren't no shots fired and we weren't in no danger. I don't know where he hightailed it."

Martin raised his eyebrows at Charles. "You think he cut and run?"

Charles said nothing. He'd been waiting for Hank to find an opportunity to desert. Ever since Castor had joined their group, the man had become withdrawn, every glance clouded in resentment. He wasn't much of a soldier and truth be told, he wasn't much of a man.

"Well, if he did, he's nothin' more than one sorry fool," said Jimmy belligerently. "Castor shows a sight more guts than he ever did."

"Yeah, did you hear about Castor capturin' a reb this mornin'?" Martin asked.

Before Felix could respond, Martin and Jimmy jumped into the story of Castor and the rebel soldier.

Felix hardly spoke a word, while Charles laughed loudly.

In truth, the emaciated soldier nearly beat Castor back to camp in his race to be taken captive.

CHAPTER 32

March blew into April. News of Lee's retreat out of Richmond during the night of April 2-3, where the rebels set fire to everything that couldn't be moved, spurred Sherman and his cavalry toward Appomattox, 90 miles from Petersburg.

The infantry was close behind, which meant that the Confederacy was closer and closer to breaking.

Even so, the Yankee advance had been laced with conflict as Lee tried again and again to break through Sherman's blockades.

It was Castor that followed Charles up to the battle line two days later. There, beside a fallen log, half-hidden by brush, they waited for the sound of the signal trumpet.

"Boss, you think ole Lee's beat out this time?"

"I'd say so, Castor, as soon as we corner him. But he's no coward. You best remember that."

"I do, Boss, I do. But when da fight is over, then means we all gets to go home?"

Charles passed a hand over his stubble chin. "Yes, it surely does. Sounds good, doesn't it?"

"An', you, Boss, you got fam'ly back home?"

"Yes, indeed I do." Charles felt a thickening in his throat. He looked the young man over carefully. "What will you do when the war is over, Castor?"

"Dunno, Boss." The boy suddenly smiled. "Get me a job. Yes, sir, dat is what I'd likes to do!"

Having never considered the enormity of Castor's choices now that he was a free man, Charles nodded. "Perhaps you can tender horses. Even the lieutenant says you're the best horse doctor he's seen in years. And look at that old mule. He looks younger every day."

Castor chuckled, embarrassed. "Yes, he do, don't he? An' he is somethin', Boss! Dat ole Boss-mule tells me his worries. I had to tie him to the cart just this mornin' just so he wouldn't follow me. Such foolishness. He's full of foolishness, dat ole mule."

The sound of the trumpet interrupted their conversation. Charles, knowing their reprieve had been short-lived, pressed the butt of his rifle to his shoulder and got to his feet. He scanned the gray line of the horizon as he inched forward. "Stay close, Castor."

"I stay right behind you, Boss!"

Charles waved his men forward and without making a sound, they followed close on his heels. It was imperative they stay within earshot of the rest of the company. The terrain was rugged and dense. "Don't stop for a minute, Castor, you hear? Where I put my feet, that's where you put yours."

He continued on, feeling Castor's body moving in line with his. It gave him great satisfaction that the boy had proved that he could soldier well. Of course, he hadn't been given a weapon, but he'd been given a cap and an over-sized jacket, which he wore proudly.

Suddenly, a series of pinging shots zipped past them. Charles instinctively jumped out of the line of fire, but as he did so, he heard a dull thud. He turned. "Castor!"

"Ah, Boss—" The boy lay, crumpled over, as if someone had sheared him across the middle and folded him in half.

"No!" boomed Charles. He dropped to the ground and pulled the boy into his arms.

"It hurts, Boss." The words gurgled up out of Castor's

mouth. "Hurts bad."

"Castor," Charles ordered, ignoring the flow of blood. "Listen to me. I'll get you back to camp."

"Ah, nah," whimpered Castor, curling up like a coiling snake. "Oh, Boss, it hurts real bad."

Charles pulled him closer. "You'll be fine, Castor, you hear me?"

Castor's eyelids fluttered as he shook his head. "I sorry, Boss. Real sorry." Jerking, he murmured, "Sweet Jesus, have mercy."

Charles pulled the boy roughly to his chest.

Peace negotiations began in earnest two days later. Facing one another in the parlor of Wilmer McLean's home, General Grant dictated the terms of surrender to General Lee. Then, on the afternoon of April 9, the final surrender was signed at the Appomattox Court House.

It was what everyone had been waiting for. It was almost time to go home.

Home: the word stuck like a thorn in Charles' side. Would Mary Elizabeth even want him back? What would the girls think of the bedraggled man that was their father?

He was a changed man, he knew, and he feared neither they nor anyone else would recognize him.

CHAPTER 33

The news swept through the camp like a hurricane. Charles was standing outside his tent, looking out over the rows of well-ordered quarters, wondering if life would ever be as well-ordered again.

Suddenly Martin rushed forward, sobbing, his words swallowed up by tears. "The President's been shot. Shot and killed!"

"What?"

"Lincoln! He's been murdered!"

It couldn't be true, thought Charles. Not Lincoln. Not the man who had sought to bring the fractured nation together again.

But it was true.

Which left the bigger question: what would happen to the fragile peace constructed at Appomattox?

It was on June 7, six weeks after Lincoln's assassination, that Charles and Martin were discharged. Dressed in full uniform, or as close to full dress as anyone could muster, the 116th, in company with other units, paraded past hundreds of people gathered along the avenues of Washington, D.C.

At the front of the column, Sherman looked magnificent on horseback.

Charles watched him from where he marched at the head of his column. He'd been given another promotion along with his discharge, which meant he'd be leaving the army as a lieutenant.

Not that it would bring him any great reward, Charles reminded himself. But the title was something he could at least offer Mary Elizabeth.

But the return to Decatur was hardly cause for celebration. He noted the shabbiness that had come over everything; obviously life here had not been easy, either.

He wondered how Mary Elizabeth and the girls had fared. Hopefully the money he'd sent had been enough.

He hurried on, then stopped when he saw the general store.

Inside he noticed two other men, like himself, thin and worn, looking to borrow or purchase something to take home. Mr. Easton, the store clerk, was shaking his head. "Boys, I'd like to loan you what you ask, but I'm as hard-put as everybody. This war cleaned me out of just about everything. I've got to have hard coin, boys, real notes. Not a by-golly or hard-time token."

The two men, turning on their heels, left the store without a word. Charles hesitated. He, too, had thought of asking for a loan, but perhaps he'd dig out the few coins he'd managed to save.

"Mr. Easton," he said, "I'm in need of a ready-made shirt. Do you stock them?" Before the clerk could respond, Charles dropped two half-dollars on the counter.

Mr. Easton smiled. "Well, Mr. Bowles, I do indeed. You know, we heard you'd been wounded a while back. Glad to see the Confederates didn't do more than wing you." He looked Charles over carefully, then bent down to retrieve several shirts. "Collars come for a nickel more, of course, but I'm sure we have something that will fit."

Charles examined the stiff fabric. The stitching was even and tidy. "Have you seen Mrs. Bowles?" he asked. He kept his voice even. "I sent word that I was coming, but of course, I had no way of knowing exactly when I'd arrive."

"I've seen Mrs. Bowles only a few times of late. She's been taking in work, I do believe. Has an eye for tailoring, she does. In fact, I bought a few of her ready-mades myself. She doesn't make men's shirts, however. These came from Springfield."

Charles nodded, keeping his surprise hidden behind his smile. He'd not thought Mary Elizabeth would have to labor. Of course, with the scarcity of everything, no doubt prices had been dear, supplies limited.

Mr. Easton allowed Charles to change in the storeroom. The stiff collar, the musty smell of fabric, and the roughness of the starched cloth against his skin reminded him of how long it'd been since he'd worn anything clean or new.

"If you'd like," suggested Mr. Easton, "you can wash up behind the store. I got a tub and a rag. Even a comb. I'm sure you'd like to spruce up for Mrs. Bowles."

"Thank you, Mr. Easton."

However, it would take more than a comb to spruce up, thought Charles. He only hoped Mary Elizabeth didn't send him packing after she got a good look at him.

CHAPTER 34

The house seemed smaller, the landscape more barren than Charles recalled. Pulling the sagging wooden gate open, he frowned; how long had this been broken?

He also noticed that no flowers bloomed in the yard, but his heart skipped a beat when he saw the front door standing ajar.

Was it his wife's voice drifting out through the doorway and down the steps?

"Girls! Supper's nearly ready, so put those dolls down. Lillian, let me wash your hands. Ida, go get some wood. Eva, help me lay out the dishes."

Hearing the soft patter of footsteps running across a wooden floor, Charles took a step sideways. He felt like a schoolboy—anxious, fidgety.

It was then that Ida danced out onto the porch. No longer a small child, her long golden curls had been brushed back and severely anchored with a thin brown ribbon. Her cherub face had lost much of its chubby softness and he wondered how much she'd suffered while he'd been gone.

She had to be eight years old, but she looked older than that.

She didn't see him at first, her mind on the chore at hand. Then she screamed, "Papa! Papa!"

Nearly tumbling down the steps, she ran to him.

Charles swept her into his arms, his voice thick. "Ida! Darling Ida."

"I knew you'd come back," she declared as she held

him fast. "I told Mama not to worry. I told her —"

Hugging her till he feared he might smother her, he felt her tears through the fabric of his new shirt.

The next few minutes seemed to kaleidoscope as she pulled him into the house.

Mary Elizabeth stood frozen to the floor, one hand on Lillian's shoulder, the other at her hip.

"Didn't I tell you, Mama? Didn't I promise he'd be home soon?" Ida cried.

Instantly, Mary Elizabeth's face changed. "Why didn't you let us know you were on your way home? Why didn't you write?"

Charles struggled for an answer. "I came, as soon as I could."

Flustered, she turned to her eldest daughter. "Ida, get a chair for your papa."

Charles sat down, but he was a stranger in a strange house.

Mary Elizabeth stiffened. As if to show him how out of place he was, she turned to Lillian and whispered to the toddler, "Sweetheart, this is your papa."

Lillian shook her head defiantly. "No!"

Mary Elizabeth spoke firmly. "Yes, dear, this is your papa."

Charles sighed. "Ah, she's frightened. Let it be, Mary Elizabeth."

Mary Elizabeth frowned. "Indeed."

At bedtime, Ida and Eva consoled the pouting Lillian as the three girls cuddled under the weight of two heavy patchwork quilts. Watching from the fireplace, Charles wished he could have at least given Lillian a hug. But she'd have nothing to do with him, only screamed if he came too close.

Mary Elizabeth kissed each of the girls, then pulled the quilts up to their chins. "Snug as three bugs," she whispered. She ran her finger along each of their brows, causing them to giggle in response. "Are you warm enough?"

Ida nodded, and Charles grimaced.

In spite of the fire burning in the fireplace, and in spite of the fact that it was June, the tiny alcove serving as the girls' bedroom was cold. Indeed, the entire house was more inadequate than he'd remembered.

"Good night, girls," said Mary Elizabeth. "Remember Papa in your prayers."

Ida glanced over at Charles. "Mama said that every night you were gone. And every morning I watched for you. Now I don't have to watch for your coming any more."

Touched by his daughter's unwavering devotion, Charles smiled. "You were in my prayers, too. Each one of you." He looked from Ida to Eva and then to Lillian. "All of you," he repeated and his glance moved to include Mary Elizabeth.

Mary Elizabeth ignored his confession. "It's quite late. Time for sleep." Picking up the lantern, she returned to the front room, her skirts rustling across the plank floor.

"It's over, Mary Elizabeth, do you hear me? And I'm home for good."

Mary Elizabeth's shrill voice startled him. "I don't know. Is a thing like war ever over? People were changed as a result of this war, Charles, and it wasn't just the soldiers who fought and died or went hungry and cried. It wasn't just them who suffered."

"I know it must have been hard for everyone."

Suddenly she slapped at her apron as if swatting a fly. "It was and now you're home. But I'm not the same woman you left behind. Did you know there were nights when I put the girls to bed with hardly more than mush or boiled potatoes in their bellies? The price of food at times was more

116

than I could afford."

"I sent you everything I could— "

"And we had more than some. Still, it's been two years. Long, hard years, Charles. Long, lonely years."

Her anger hit its mark. "What more can I say? If there was a snowball's chance I could change what happened, I would."

He felt a cold rush of fear run down the back of his neck. Wouldn't she let her guard down, even for a moment?

"Enough," she moaned. "You are such a dreamer, Charles. Such grand notions you had." She pulled her apron off over her head. "But the war went the way of every war, and it's not over yet. With Mr. Lincoln hardly cold in the grave, and the South scrapping to get its feet on the ground, it's going to be a long, long summer and, I'd wager, a long time before real peace comes to this land."

CHAPTER 35

Charles could not find adequate work. There were more laborers than jobs and certainly no call for a schoolmaster; indeed, he'd been replaced by a dour, elderly woman who ran the school and the children more efficiently than he ever could.

Even the Disbrows, though glad to have him home, had no work for Charles. They'd leased out their farm to a stout Missourian whose two sons and wife provided any labor they needed.

Days faded into weeks as Charles took on odd jobs. But a strange emptiness had replaced any joy he'd felt in coming home. It was as if he were outside, watching Mary Elizabeth and the girls as they laughed and chatted and continued on in their simple life.

He'd have to find a way to make a difference.

With that in mind, on a bright August morning, he made his decision.

Mary Elizabeth was in the kitchen, her hair tied back, her face pinched and wet as she kneaded dough into loaves of bread. She'd managed to wrangle more business by offering to bake for a handful of well-to-do folks in town. Added to the tidy sum she collected for her tailor-made clothes, she was keeping the Bowles' family out of debt.

Charles reached for a cup on the shelf to her left. "I've decided we will move to Iowa." When she didn't respond, he went on. "There we will build a farm."

Mary Elizabeth wiped her brow with her forearm, her lips drawn in a frown.

He raised the coffeepot, keeping his voice pleasant. "Iowa. Think of it. We'll have a great start there. With new townships springing up everywhere, we'll have the chance to make a real living."

Again, Mary Elizabeth ignored him. Slapping one chunk of dough into a round loaf, she dropped it on a large cooking stone.

Charles set the pot of steaming coffee back down and took a steadying breath. He couldn't lose his temper. "We both know I've become a millstone around your neck," he said. "I can't even draw a decent wage as a hand. Don't you see? There's nothing left for me around here. We've got to move on."

Mary Elizabeth picked up a rag and dabbed at her cheeks before sighing. "Iowa?"

"New Oregon is what they're calling the settlement. Several families from around here have already headed out."

She returned to her balls of dough and quickly shaped another loaf.

"Please, turn around, Mary Elizabeth! I am still your husband."

Mary Elizabeth chuckled sardonically. "I can't argue that."

He exhaled slowly. "I know I can't make up for what's happened. I can't change the past. But we are moving to New Oregon, and if you're going to let it stick in your craw, well, then, go right ahead."

They set out for northeastern Iowa early in spring, but did not go directly to New Oregon. Mary Elizabeth, realizing she was with child, insisted they find a settled town until the baby came.

The birth of Arian was another arduous battle for Mary Elizabeth, one that left her weak and depressed. But Charles was overjoyed to have a son and immediately took over his care. Ida and Eva gleefully assisted him and even Lillian warmed to the squeals of her baby brother.

When the day arrived to move to New Oregon, Mary Elizabeth remained stoic, but withdrawn, as she packed the last of the boxes and the baby into the wagon Charles had borrowed from a neighbor.

The girls climbed in, Ida taking the spot nearest their father. Eva flopped down behind her, tears welling up in her eyes. "You always get to sit with Papa."

Charles took his seat and turned to smile at his two eldest daughters. "Everyone will have a turn to ride up front," he whispered.

Eva smiled and stuck her tongue out at Ida.

"Enough," sighed Mary Elizabeth.

In exaggerated fashion, Charles slapped the rumps of the four gray mules with his reins, then called out, "Giddy-yap. We got miles to go, you no-accounts."

Ida squealed with delight, and Eva's disappointment vanished.

But the mules only took a few steps forward before stopping to nibble along the roadway.

"Stubborn and slow, aren't they?" murmured Mary Elizabeth.

"Like some folks, you might add?" smiled Charles. "At least they're reliable."

Eva tapped Charles' shoulder. "May I sit with you and hold the reins, Papa? It's my turn."

He glanced at Ida. "It is, indeed."

Ida frowned.

Mary Elizabeth shook her head. "It's much too dangerous. We've enough to worry about with the load swaying this way and that."

"I won't let her do more than tickle their backsides."

"I don't like it, Charles." Mary Elizabeth patted Arian who had started fussing.

"Please, Mama?"

"No," snapped Mary Elizabeth and she reached around and patted Eva's arm. "You stay right where you are."

Charles caught Mary Elizabeth's glance. "Let her take a turn. Ida, switch places with your sister."

Climbing between Charles and Mary Elizabeth, who held Arian firmly against her shoulder, Ida grinned. She took the reins and clucked loudly.

Charles patted her hands. "Whoa, girl. Just a gentle swat, enough to let them know who's in charge. Remember, sometimes it's wise to show your strength, and sometimes it's wiser to withhold it."

"Huh," mumbled Mary Elizabeth as she shifted in her seat.

CHAPTER 36

Around the tiny settlement of New Oregon, the country was empty and flat, dotted only by occasional groves of trees or stands of brush. There was not much to recommend it except its clear, unfettered view.

Charles began to wonder if he'd traveled even further from his dream. "It looks— promising," he said as they entered the tiny town. He pulled up to the clapboard mercantile. "I'll ask around. Our place can't be too far from here."

Mary Elizabeth said nothing, but her expression told him that the place was more than likely too far from everywhere.

Once inside the general store, Charles looked around. Two men leaned against the nearby plank counter, one a towering fellow with dark complexion, the other a slender, bearded man. The taller man was shuffling a deck of cards.

"Hello," said Charles.

"Welcome to New Oregon," said the slender man, "a town destined to be the next Promised Land."

"That's good," smiled Charles. "We've been on the road for many days, not unlike the Israelites of old."

The slender man chuckled. "But not lost, I hope."

"Hopefully not," returned Charles. "In truth, I have a deed entitling me to 160 acres somewhere around here. Can you help me locate it?"

"Certainly. By the way, my name's Samuel Smith."

When Charles emerged, he was smiling. He climbed

onto the wagon seat and patted Mary Elizabeth's folded hands. "I just met our neighbor. He said there's a cabin already built on our land, just waiting for the next family to move in."

But the abandoned cabin they found turned out to be hardly more than a lean-to. Considerably smaller than the cabin they'd rented on the Disbrow farm, the kitchen was a stove recessed against one wall of the main room, the only real room of the cabin. It was dark, lit by a narrow window situated on the easterly wall, so that even the bright afternoon sunshine did not shine in.

Charles wondered if there would be room enough for Mary Elizabeth's three spindle-backed chairs and maple rocker. Glancing at her as she stood with hands on her hips, a frown creasing her pale face, he knew she wondered the same thing.

Behind a ragged slip of a curtain, she discovered the sleeping quarters. "There won't be room for the girls, the baby, or our bed in this space."

"Oh, Mary Elizabeth, this is but temporary. I'll set to work first thing."

"And I won't wait even that long." Stepping out onto the porch, she called to the girls. "Bring me the broom and a bucket!"

Directing Eva and Ida to sweep, Mary Elizabeth went to work washing down the cabin. It took more than three hours. When she finished, perspiration lined her upper lip and curled the long strands of loosened hair about her ears. "It's not perfect, but it'll have to do."

The girls flopped on the floor beside Arian, who slept in his cradle.

Charles, his arms full of the bedding that Mary Elizabeth had set him to fetch, shook his head. He nodded to the rocker he'd brought in earlier. "Come, relax. I'll rustle up some kindling and build us a fire."

But the chimney was plugged, and because he realized it belatedly, smoke and ash billowed out into the room, covering the floorboards with a powdery film.

Mary Elizabeth cast him a hateful glance. "What were you doing outside all this time if not cleaning the chimney?" Throwing open the front door, she fanned the thick black cloud with her apron. "Go get the broom, Ida. We'll have to start again."

Ida whined, "I'm tired."

"And so am I, child," snapped Mary Elizabeth.

jumped up off the floor. "I'll get it, Mama." Then she turned to her father. "I don't like this house at all, Papa. It's too small. It's dark. And it smells."

"It's a sight better than no house at all," he said stubbornly, and dropped the bedding onto the ash-covered floor.

CHAPTER 37

It wasn't long before Charles recognized that the move to New Oregon had been another mistake. Hiram hadn't been able to make the move after all, leaving Charles to work the farming alone. Without implements or adequate provisions, he'd abandoned the idea of building a farm entirely.

In addition, incidental work was as hard to find in Iowa as it had been in Illinois, and it was equally hard for Mary Elizabeth to take in work. Few could afford a seamstress and with no friends or relatives nearby to care for Arian or help with the girls, she couldn't go far. Before long, her frame of mind and health began to suffer.

As a result, everyone suffered.

It was clear to Charles that he'd have to find a way to make some money, but where to begin?

"It'd puzzle a half dozen Philadelphia lawyers to unriddle this nation's present state of affairs," he confided to Samuel Smith several weeks later. "I'm not the only soldier who's come home to find no job."

Sam stroked the spindly hairs of his red-orange beard as he settled himself beside Charles. The two men had agreed to oversee the children who splashed noisily along the river's shallows. "And it's no thanks to the federal government. Offerin' up land for nigras just don't seem right when it takes jobs away from the men who fought the war. I'll wear this ball forever." He pointed to his hip and the wound he'd suffered at Sharpsburg. In truth, the ball had saved Sam's life, but Charles didn't remind him of that fact today.

"I tell you honestly," continued Sam, rubbing his hip,

"it's enough to boil a man's blood. Sure, I've got plenty to keep me busy, but I look around and see these nigras moving north and last week, one walked right into Henderson's smithy and got work. Why didn't he hire you? We been to town any number of times and that skin-flint never offered you a thing."

Charles let his gaze wander to where Eva and Ida were scrambling up Sam's boys' rope swing. He hadn't told Mary Elizabeth that Eva could now climb onto Ida's shoulders and grab the knot.

Nor had he told her that Eva had slipped more than once from the rope to crash into the water. The afternoon outings had become the high point of his days as well as the girls'. They eagerly waited for the hour when he'd walk them down the lane that wound around to the river's edge.

"I suppose Henderson's right in assuming neither of us are equal to the task. Look at Winston. He's stouter than three men." Charles picked up a small round stone and flicked it into the water.

Eva shrieked as water splashed across her face.

He turned to Sam. "I don't begrudge a good man like Winston a job. You gotta admit he's strong and able."

"Well," drawled Sam, "Given time, most white men could stand up to Winston or any nigra."

Charles let himself fall back against the rocky soil, then pulled his hat down over his eyes. Sam was a fool, truth be told. Old Winston was a far better man than either he or Sam. A slave all his life, he'd left Alabama with a wife and four small children and been willing to take on the jobs nobody else wanted. And Henderson was a bear of a man, not easy to get along with. That in itself spoke volumes about Winston's abilities.

As the sun waned, Charles felt his eyes grow heavy. Suddenly, in the distance, he heard a commotion.

"Papa!" came the small cry.

Charles scrambled to his feet, squinting against the

126

afternoon's glare.

"There!" shouted Sam.

He glanced down the shoreline, then spotted the top of his small daughter's head bobbing up and down like a cork.

"Eva!"

He rushed to the water's edge and dove in.

She was trying to stay afloat. "Papa," she gasped.

In three strokes he reached her and instantly slipped his arms around her tiny body. As he raised her up, he felt for the sandy river bottom, then carried her to shore. "Papa's got you, Eva. Papa's got you."

When he reached the sandy shallows, he exhaled slowly.

Eva wiggled out of his grasp. "Put me down, Papa."

Sam rushed over, his own gaze raking the river's edge. "Where are the boys, Eva? Where's Ida? I don't see the others anywhere."

With both feet planted firmly in the sand, Ida pointed downriver. "George told Ida he saw a beaver dam and he knew how to catch us a beaver. But he wouldn't take me. I wanted to see the beaver, too, Papa."

Sam turned and began yelling in the direction the children had gone. "You fool boys! Get back here, now!"

Charles smiled at Eva. "We'll find you a beaver another day, sweetheart."

"You promise, Papa?"

Mary Elizabeth was furious when Charles returned with the wet and chilled Eva and a pouting Ida. "How could you be so thoughtless?" she demanded of Ida who stood in the center of the cabin, arms folded against her chest defiantly. "How could you think your sister could manage on her own?" Then she turned to Charles. "But you—"

"That's enough said," Charles interrupted. He was not about to abide a second scolding from his wife. He'd given her time to unleash her fury when they'd first walked up the path, but he would not take any more of it. He'd been as scared as any man could be, more than he cared to admit. "Let's get these girls to bed. Where's Lillian? And Arian?"

"Asleep, thank the Lord," returned Mary Elizabeth. "Especially since Arian started up another cough today. And he only took a trifle of milk." She began rubbing Eva down with the old quilt she had taken off the girls' cot, not wanting Charles to see the gathering fear she harbored.

It had been enough to worry day in and day out over Arian and his health. Now, it seemed she'd have to worry about the girls' welfare, too. She glanced up at her husband and frowned. He was oblivious, she realized, to the impact his decisions had on her and the children.

Just like a man.

She watched him move to the fire. He sat down and closed his eyes.

She finished rubbing Eva down and after tucking her in, followed her husband to the fire. She cleared her throat.

"From now on, Charles, the girls and Arian will stay here—with me. No more water holes or rope swings, no more gallivanting around the countryside. Do you understand?" She heaved a sigh and cast him a hard look.

Charles' jaw tightened as the color in his face faded.

CHAPTER 38

For a week, Arian's condition fluctuated. From morning 'til night, he lay in Mary Elizabeth's lap, refusing milk and hardly stirring as Mary Elizabeth rocked him, tears falling down her cheeks. The chair's well-worn rockers squeaked against the cabin's uneven floorboards.

Charles watched, unable to voice his own fears. And what could he do? Every attempt to console his wife was rebuked. Even Eva and Ida refused to come near him, running away whenever he called them to his side.

"Mama says bringing us to this 'God-forsaken place is what made Arian sick," Ida had sobbed, balling her fists at her hips.

Charles didn't argue. She most likely spoke the plain and simple truth.

Early the next day, however, Mary Elizabeth ordered Charles to fetch the doctor. "I don't care if I have to stitch his britches for a month to pay him back," she snarled. "Just make him come. Do you hear me, Charles? Don't let him put you off, not even for an hour."

Nodding as he pulled his coat from its hook, Charles headed out the door.

Unfortunately a storm was moving in quickly. Already great gray clouds were rolling in like tumbleweeds across the horizon and thunder rumbled in the distance. Charles slapped his horse into a gallop as the wind whirled around him.

When Charles finally reached town, it was nearly noon.

Frank Gibbs, a no-account gambler who spent more time wandering alleys than dealing cards, stepped up to greet Charles as he dallied his horse along the railing in front of Doc Conklin's office. "He went out to Sam Smith's place, over out your way. If you hurry back, you may just cross his path."

Frustrated, Charles looked back the way he'd come. "Thanks."

"You bet," said Frank. He dropped down into one of the chairs positioned under the eaves of the doctor's tiny office and watched as Charles beat feet back out of town.

The doctor followed Charles home, but it was well past suppertime when they pulled up to the tiny cabin. Through the single-paned window, the amber glow of the lantern cast an eerie halo around the small room.

Charles pushed the front door open and rushed in, the doctor at his heels.

"Where've you been?" demanded Mary Elizabeth. Her eyes swollen, her cheeks puffy, she gathered up the folds of her apron and the bundle cradled there.

"Sam's boys took sick, too. I ended up riding to town and back to get him."

Dr. Conklin looked down at Mary Elizabeth. "Charles says the baby's ill."

"Ill?" sobbed Mary Elizabeth. "Not anymore. He's dead." Turning her tear-streaked face up to Charles, she opened the envelope of her apron. "Your son."

The words were a knife in Charles' gut. "Mary Elizabeth, I—"

"Don't touch him!" She jerked back, eyes flashing. "Just leave us alone!"

Dr. Conklin stepped between them. "Don't be blaming your husband, Mrs. Bowles. The child has always been frail—"

She shook her head.

"Not every child is meant to live. At least not in this world," he whispered.

CHAPTER 39

Mary Elizabeth's decision to leave a month after Arian's death stunned Charles.

How could a woman leave her husband? It was preposterous.

"Then you go," she said, her eyes piercing the protective barrier he had begun to construct around his heart.

"Me?"

"Why not? You're good at leaving, Charles, and don't tell me you haven't already considered it. Even Eva and Ida know it's time for you to go."

He took a step forward, but she held up her hand. Her voice reflected little emotion. "The girls and I will return to Illinois, at least for awhile. You can contact us through your sister. Certainly the girls will want to hear from you, at least on occasion."

Charles took a slow deep breath. He knew he deserved her anger, but this? How could they part like this?

"Oh, Charles, let's don't make this harder than it is. I know you thought the war would bring some grand opportunity to get ahead. You've always been a dreamer. But when you came home, things were, just, different. I was different. You were different."

"Not so different," he said.

She frowned. "Very different. But to be fair, after Arian was born, I thought we could make things work. At least I hoped we could—" She sighed and shook her head.

Charles broke in. "Then why not now? It's foolish not

to try."

"Say what you like, Charles, if it makes you feel better, but I'm taking the girls and that's that." She looked away. "I do have something for you. Two gifts the girls and I bought one day in town, before Arian—. We had thought to give them to you at Christmas, but now—"

"You make it pretty hard on a fellow, Mary Elizabeth," whispered Charles. "I know I've done a lot of things wrong—"

Again Mary Elizabeth raised her hand. This time she shook her head. "Nothing more, Charles. Please." Then, without any further sign of emotion, she walked over to the fireplace mantle and opened the wooden box in which she'd often stored her stitching. She removed a small Bible and a pocket watch. "It's not particularly fancy," she said, holding out her hand, "but maybe it will get you where you want to go on time."

The watch felt cold against his fingers.

"Read the inscription. The girls thought of it."

Mary Elizabeth stepped back as he turned the watch over and read the simple words aloud. "Father. Husband."

"I know you are not a man of considerable faith, but I believe the Bible is something that might give you inspiration, should you ever need it." Mary Elizabeth looked up then, and he saw the tears pooling in her eyes.

He felt wooden, overcome by his own sadness. "Please—"

She turned away. "I don't know, Charles. Perhaps in a years, maybe more, my heart will soften. And mayhap by then you will know what it is you want out of life. If so, you may write and tell us." She glanced at him over her shoulder. "You are a good man, Charles."

He smirked, "No—I am hardly a good man."

"Well, for what it's worth, it wasn't only you that failed. I had a hand in it." Her voice softened. "But Arian.

Arian was my last child and my only son. I have nothing more to give you."

As he fondled the soft, smooth surface of the watch, wondering how he could change her mind, Charles took a slow deliberate breath and sighed.

He knew when he'd been beaten.

CHAPTER 40

From Last Chance Gulch to Prickly Pear and Boulder Valley, Charles roamed, hoping to find a claim worth pursuing. None yielded more than dust, however, so he continued to trade one claim for another.

For a spell he worked with a partner. But the man had been lazy.

More than that, he turned out to be a thief.

Charles could never prove it, of course, but when a pair of well-dressed men arrived with a penned piece of paper they declared was their deed to his claim, his partner admitted that he'd failed to file the original papers when he'd gone to town to do so.

"I was waitin' on the mail and Wells Fargo," he murmured apologetically, his tobacco-stained lips flapping against yellowed teeth. "You knowed I was waitin' to hear from my wife. And these men, well, they swindled me out of the deed whilst we was playin' cards. I jest didn't have the heart to tell ye before this, Charles."

Days later, Charles found himself in Helena, in a poker game with half a dozen drunken miners. It was past midnight, but he had no better place to go, even at this hour.

With a curt nod to each of the men, he placed a stack of chips on the table along with a small glass of whisky and a bowl of hard-boiled eggs.

After an hour, Charles was bored. He thought of cashing in when the young man sitting opposite spoke up.

"I'm lookin' for a partner," the boy said.

Everyone, except Charles, laughed.

Charles frowned; though not more than twenty, the young miner bore the harried look of a tired, old man. His face was narrow and drawn down at the corners of his mouth. One front tooth was missing, giving him a lop-sided expression. Long arms extended well past tattered sleeves.

"Partnering' can be dangerous," replied the man sitting next to Charles.

Charles didn't say anything; after all, the boy's business was his own.

"But you need a partner in these parts," the young man said.

"And you ain't got one?" asked the dealer. "Surely you didn't reef him and leave him to the buzzards?"

The men round the table and those standing nearby laughed.

"If you can't look out for yourself, you ought to lickety-split back home," piped a cowboy at the bar. "Your mama's probably pining' away for you this very minute." Picking up a cheroot, he rolled it in his fingertips and looked around. "You know, I get awful tired of tripping' over every stupid kid that finds himself lost or broke."

The young man turned to face the stranger. "This here conversation wasn't directed at you."

The dealer interrupted him. "Please, gentlemen, place your bets."

The young man picked up the cards in front of him. His pale blue eyes never left the hand as he sorted through it. "My partner died last week. Couldn't take the cold no more. So, like I said, I'm lookin' for a partner."

Charles ran a finger along the surface of his moustache, keeping his focus on the cards he'd been dealt. This could be a winning hand, if he kept his mind on the game.

The young man discarded one card.

136

The dealer and the last man at the table discarded three.

Picking up the two cards the dealer flipped at him, Charles said, "I heard some color was found in a place called Spring Gulch. Maybe you could find a partner there."

The young man picked up his card before looking up. "Mister, if you're interested in Spring Gulch, I'd partner up with you. My name's Cory McCutcheon." Leaning back, he absently repeated his name.

Charles frowned. He didn't want to partner with anyone, let alone some boy.

Before Charles could respond, however, Cory blurted, "Gentlemen, I declare I seen this hand already." He turned his steady gaze on the dealer. "I'm sure of it."

The dealer raised his eyebrows. "You're saying I rigged the deck?"

Cory glanced around before drawing himself up. "Yes, I do believe I am. You know, it couldn't be a coincidence that this is the second time I've seen these cards."

Charles cleared his throat. "Chance is a funny thing, Cory. Never can tell when the odds will roll over."

The young man leaned forward. "But I ain't never been that lucky, you see. One way or t'other."

"Perhaps it'd be better to play the hand dealt to you," offered Charles. This wasn't the place for a kid like Cory to display such grim courage.

The man who'd asked for three cards tapped his fingers against the backs of his fanned cards. "This is a friendly game, boy, just a game amongst gentlemen."

"Don't know how friendly it is," mumbled Cory, his eyebrows drawn down over his eyes, "or if there's even a gentlemen amongst us. But I can tell you, my daddy didn't raise no fool."

The dealer chuckled. "Mayhap your daddy would say you just landed forked end up." He pointed to the place where Cory's chips should have been stacked. "You've lost just about everything you put out in front of you tonight. It might be better if you high-tail it home before you lose your shirt."

Suddenly, without warning, the table tumbled forward, and Cory McCutcheon jumped to his feet. The rest of the players scrambled after the clattering chips and coin.

"I just lost the best hand I seen in a month of Sundays!" howled the man who had tried to pacify Cory. He was shuffling through the mess of cards splayed across the floor.

Charles, having jumped clear of the confusion, kept his eyes on Cory. The boy seemed not to understand the trouble he'd just spawned.

Instead, his eyes glittered as brightly as the barrel of the small gun now pointed at the dealer. With hammer pulled back, he snarled, "I told you, my daddy didn't raise no—"

Before he could finish his statement, two shots rang out.

Shaking his head, the cowboy who'd challenged him earlier slipped his own pistol back into his belt. "Plum foolish," he said, glancing around at the crowd gathered around. "No doubt about it," he added. "He just wasn't goin' to listen to reason."

No one else said a word.

Charles knelt beside the young man and slipped an arm under his shoulders. "Why'd you go and draw your gun?"

Clasping his stomach, blood oozing through his fingers, Cory whispered, "Well, like I said, mister, I ain't never been that lucky. One way or t'other." Then his head dropped to his chest.

CHAPTER 41

Charles stopped beside a small creek and knelt in the ankle-high grass lining the bank. The morning dew penetrated the fabric of his ragged pants as he leaned over to scoop up water with his hands.

After a long drink, he sat back and surveyed his surroundings. A sandy cut bank rose up from the edge of the creek like a broken wall, while waves of soft green rolled off to the west like ocean swells. A trio of cottonwoods stood like gray sentinels over the empty plain.

He hadn't stopped moving since leaving Helena two weeks ago, and without understanding why, the boy's death still haunted him. That others were floundering through life was more troubling than comforting.

"Life is a strange dream. Or perhaps, in truth, it's but a nightmare," he said and closed his eyes. He shuddered as the brisk morning air washed over him like morning ablutions.

He stood up and moved on. He had to shake off this cloud of foreboding. Like the boy, he knew his father had not raised a fool, and yet, what a fool he'd been to believe his aspirations were achievable.

The Devil danced in empty pockets and his had been empty for far too long.

Charles entered the makeshift town late the next day. Entering the sod building, which called itself a saloon, he had to squint to make out the human forms hidden in the shadows of the narrow room.

The bartender smiled. "Welcome, friend. We haven't

seen a new face in days. You looking for a drink?"

Charles nodded. "Water."

A hearty chuckle greeted his request. Charles turned. Two men sat at the table nearest him.

"Water?" echoed the first.

"The water round these parts is more bitter than the ale," said the second.

Charles turned back to the bartender. "Water," he repeated. "And a bottle."

He finished off the gray liquid that passed as water before picking up the bottle with his left hand. "Is this game private?" he asked.

"Not at all," returned the first man. "We'd welcome your attendance. I've just about taken all of Henry's money anyway."

Charles sat down and removed the last of the cash he had.

The second man, Henry, glanced at the bills. "That's not much of a grubstake, Mister."

Charles moved the bottle to the center of the table. "I'll bet you this bottle that I'll double it in two hands."

"Done," said Henry, with a smile to his neighbor. "I could use a stiff drink. How 'bout you, Grant?"

"Sounds good."

Charles doubled his money in the first hand, and after two hours, he pushed back from the table and smiled. "Gentlemen, it's been a pleasure."

"Well, I won't say as I ain't glad you're stepping away," returned Henry solemnly.

"In parting, sirs, I'll leave you the rest of the bottle."

Grant smiled. "I'll play for your half, Henry. You don't have anything else to wager."

"Not on your life," snapped Henry. "I need it to drown in."

Charles excused himself once more then nodded to the bartender and left quickly, the money he'd won shoved into his pockets. He had enough now to book passage on the next stage for California.

He couldn't say that he wasn't relieved to be on his way west.

CHAPTER 42

A bustling city of thousands now, San Francisco was alive with activity. Hardly more than a beachfront settlement in 1850, it had grown substantially in the years he'd been away. Even now, three months after his arrival, Charles marveled at its color and verve.

The avenues swarmed with men of every sort: rag-tag, sophisticated, dark-skinned, red-skinned. There were hordes of Celestials, too, pushing carts or hauling loads across their shoulders. And women, everywhere. Neatly dressed or bawdy, no doubt many could be had for a price.

Wagons and carriages clattered along cobbled streets, as did horse-drawn streetcars. And everywhere, the smell of fish, rancid oil and smoke permeated the damp air that clung to the city's rooftops.

Charles adjusted his duster and continued up Telegraph Hill. From there, he liked to study the ships tied up along the docks, many having just come from far-away places. Someday he'd journey abroad—when time, money, and opportunity came together.

He made his way to a tavern set back from the main street and chose a corner table. Though he rarely drank much, he always ordered a bottle; it attracted attention and that usually led to a modest game of chance. And, as much as he disliked gambling, it had kept him flush. Even the clothes he wore today had been purchased with what he'd won at faro last week.

However, he was bored with this life of relative ease. He longed for something more exciting, more challenging.

More dangerous, his father or Mary Elizabeth would have said.

For a moment, he felt the wash of regret. Perhaps they'd known more about his character than he, for surely he coveted something that would stir his blood.

As two hard-luck miners stumbled past him, he pulled out a deck of playing cards and fanned them. "Gentlemen," he said, "let me buy you a drink."

"Well, I'll be," returned one. "Ain't you as right as a trivet. Thank ye kindly! Jacob, take a sit. Let's see what this gentleman is about."

Several weeks later, Charles found himself packing a valise and boarding a stage for Sonora. What fate would bring his way, he didn't know, but he was willing to play out his hand, and Sonora was as good a place as any to start.

After checking into a small inn, Charles descended the steps and entered a small parlor where a young serving girl greeted him. She offered him a glass of lemonade.

"You can't be just a miner," she suggested, her gaze taking in Charles' trim suit and walking stick.

Though dusty from traveling, he knew he looked stylish. "I am, what one might call, a mining engineer." He'd practiced that line on the ride into town and it now rolled off his tongue perfectly.

"I thought so," said the girl. "We don't get many important people 'round here. I surely hope your room will be satisfactory, Mr. Bolton."

Charles smiled. He was enjoying the masquerade. "Well, Miss, I do appreciate your kind regard." Handing her his empty glass, he tapped the edge of his bowler before strolling out of the inn.

Ironically, he felt at peace with the world for the first time in months. And that, in spite of what he'd been toying with for the last several days, was especially satisfying.

When he reached the site he'd spotted on his way into town, he stopped and surveyed his surroundings. He'd learned from his days at war that a man must appreciate the challenges and advantages of any situation. Assessing this situation would prevent him from making any costly errors in judgment.

And, hadn't he always prided himself on his good judgment?

He reached into his coat pocket and felt for the smooth surface of his pocket watch. He removed it, fingering the inscription carefully. It reminded him too starkly of Mary Elizabeth and the girls.

He shoved the regrets aside. There was no helping what was past. Hadn't he spent the last twenty years snatching at dreams that either belonged to others or remained far out of his reach? Hadn't he tried to live a life of respectability, despite all that had been taken from him?

All the more reason for taking what should have been his.

He glanced at the time. It was quarter past six.

Catching his breath, he slipped the watch back into his pocket and adjusted his derby. The summer sun was rising behind him, and he knew it would cast the perfect light across the approaching grade.

He leaned over his bedroll and removed a dusty flour sack. It fit snugly over his hat and face. Not just a mask, it created the illusion that he was taller than he was. He fiddled with the torn eyeholes until he could see in every direction. Satisfied, he slid his bedroll into the nearby brush and set his axe behind a large rock.

He felt the rush of blood to his face. His hands trembled slightly. But he didn't have time for second thoughts. He'd come too far.

CHAPTER 43

Grinding wheels and pounding hoofs startled him. Inhaling, he listened for the horses lunging up the steep ascent. The horses would be tired, for, though the worst part was over, the stage had to crest Funk Hill. Hopefully it would be enough to slow the team to a walk.

Charles adjusted his mask, took up his sawed-off shotgun and stepped out from behind the boulder. He took a slow, steady breath before raising the gun to his shoulder.

The driver, still unaware of him, was leaning forward on the plank seat, slouch hat tipped over one brow, gloved hands wrapped around and tugging on heavy rawhide reins. His eyes widened when he spotted Charles.

Charles immediately moved into the path of the lead horse, causing it to rear back nervously. He raised his eyes to meet the hard glance of the driver who jerked on his reins and hollered, "Whoa!" He knew the driver wouldn't reach for his gun.

A good driver never shot over his animals' backs.

"Please throw down the express box," Charles called out, his voice hardly more than a whisper.

The horses stamped nervously, their lathered shoulders and flanks quivering against their harness. The mud-wagon rocked and creaked on its axles, an eerie sound in the heavy silence.

Suddenly he spotted a man's face leaning out the side window of the carriage. He swung his gun so that it was leveled at the stranger. He lowered his voice. "Stay inside. Don't try anything. The rest of my men are just behind those trees."

The man disappeared into the coach, and Charles thought he could hear the sound of a woman or child crying. He hadn't reckoned on any passengers.

He turned back to the driver.

Hunched over, the man remained tense. One leather-clad hand rested against the brake, the other clutched the reins. His eyes, heavily-browed and closely set, were all that moved as Charles took a step forward.

"I said throw down the express box."

The driver kicked the box over the side and it thudded to the ground, dust billowing up around it. Charles moved closer, just as a lady's purse also landed in the dirt. He snatched it up and threw it back through the open window. "I don't want your money," he yelled, "only what Wells Fargo owes me."

"You're a fool," drawled the driver. "They'll send detectives and a posse after you soon as we reach town."

Charles raised his shotgun to his shoulder once more. This was not going as smoothly as he'd hoped. He gathered his nerve and shouted, "So they will. I wouldn't expect anything less. Now drive on before one of my boys gets edgy."

The driver glanced around, then slapped the team into a trot. "Get on up!"

Charles breathed a sigh of relief as he watched the team and wagon disappear into the distance.

Tucking the shotgun under one arm, he dragged the treasure box back behind the boulder where he'd left his axe. It opened with two heavy blows, but not before he heard the sound of hooves once more pounding up the grade.

He eased forward, shotgun ready. Up the grade lumbered a second stage.

He'd not figured on such good fortune.

Mask still in place, he waited until the driver spotted him before stepping out into the road.

"Express box," he called out. He took a slow, deep breath and held aim on the driver's startled face. He couldn't let the man see how undone his unexpected arrival had made him.

The driver steadied his team and shook his head. "I ain't got no strong box," he said. "I'm only carrying passengers. You can take a look-see if you want."

Charles hesitated. Once more he noted the head of a man and a woman peering out from inside the coach. He took a step back. "Be on your way, then," he yelled. "But my men'll be down your backside if you try anything."

"I don't want no trouble, Mister! No trouble at all!"

As the driver gave his team the signal to move, Charles sighed. "Trouble ain't so easy to stay away from, when it's riding your tail."

CHAPTER 44

Within the week, news of the holdup had made San Francisco headlines. A $250 reward was even being offered by Wells, Fargo & Company, a sum totaling more than what had been stolen.

Charles couldn't help but chuckle. "You think the man's cold-blooded?" he asked his landlady. She had read most of the article aloud and now repeated the number of agents Wells, Fargo & Company had sent out to the camps. "You think he's dangerous?"

"Most definitely," returned Mrs. Smyth. She held up the front page and frowned. "Any man such as this who would steal from strangers is dangerous and deserves imprisonment, maybe even hanging. My own husband shot a thief when he tried to rob one of our tenants last year. On his deathbed, he was, too, poor John, but he shot the scoundrel when he tried to slip out our bedroom window. The fool never saw my husband, hiding under the covers. A man to behold, even at the end, he was."

"That does beat all," said Charles. He was certainly glad poor John Smyth was no longer around. He supposed Mrs. Smyth kept a loaded gun under her bed, as well.

Two weeks later Charles moved to a new boarding-house on Second Street. It was centrally located, offered larger rooms, and the landlady was a quiet, demure woman.

He paid for two months' rent and hired the landlady's young son to run errands for him. Today the boy had taken his shirts down to the nearest laundry. The boy brought home a small red ticket scratched with strange symbols.

"You're to take this when you want your shirts back, Mr. Bolton. They don't give 'em out otherwise."

"How many days 'til they're ready?" Charles handed the boy a penny for his trouble.

"I don't know," said the boy. "I couldn't make out what they said." He pocketed the coin with a smile. "I'd be pleased to get them in a day or two, if you want me to."

Though it was a luxury, Charles had discovered that dressing well was one of life's necessities. It not only added to his image as a successful mining engineer, it brought him greater respect from faro dealers and acquaintances all over the city. Just today he'd been invited to a soiree at one of the finer hotels.

Indeed, in San Francisco, it was a man's coin, not his name or reputation that garnered respect.

"Hey, C.E.!"

Charles turned at the sound of the familiar nickname, but the restaurant's foyer was crowded and smoke-filled. Charles angled his way through the throng of patrons before reaching the police captain who stood with hat in hand.

Charles held out his right hand. "Good afternoon, Captain. May I buy you a cup of coffee? I've just finished dinner, but I could sit while you take yours."

"Thanks, but not today. I'm on my way out. We've been especially busy lately, as well you know. Just today Wells, Fargo & Company asked us to join the hunt for their shotgun-toting, gentleman stage bandit."

'You mean the fellow who held up the Copperopolis stage some weeks back?"

"The same. It now seems the man acted alone. But with no description and the trail stone cold, I can't do a thing. Besides, I've got thieves a-plenty to hunt down round here. And why would the thief hide in the city? He probably high-tailed it deeper into hill country."

Charles listened politely. "Well," he nodded, "good luck. I hope you find your scoundrel."

"I'd have better luck finding a pig in a poke."

"Well, no doubt he'll surface again and then you'll get a second chance."

"Huh. I count the thief more coward than bully."

CHAPTER 45

The summer of '75 proved a difficult time for San Franciscans. Fear and speculation had been fanned by frequent newspaper editorials condemning the integrity of Billy Ralston's Bank of California as well as the scarcity of hard coin. When stock prices fell, investors began to panic.

On Friday, August 27, both stock exchanges closed down. Bank clerks could only shrug their shoulders as they closed their windows. "Nothing to pay with," they said. "You'll have to take it up with the boss. Can't help you today."

The city was thrown into a state of chaos.

Charles knew his luck had held out. He had pulled out the last of his bank deposits weeks earlier and had buried them instead at the foot of David's grave.

Today he would collect a portion of it.

"Little brother," he whispered, shoving dirt back into the hole he'd dug, "you have once more come to my rescue. No doubt, if you were here today, you'd be saving me from myself."

He sat down on his haunches and sighed. "But I fear it would have been a lost cause."

Summer edged into fall with hardly more than a wind-storm, but winter followed with pounding rain and bitter cold temperatures.

On a rainy December day, Charles boarded a steamer to Marysville. The rain had made the trip miserable, but bad weather would make a holdup easier to pull off. Any driver worth his salt would be wary of driving his horses down a slick side hill or across a narrow bridge.

He entered the small hotel he'd spotted on his last trip and dropped his valise at the clerk's counter. "A room, please," he said, removing his hat and shaking it against his leg. "And a bath."

"A real gully washer," returned the clerk. "Sign in. I got a room at the top of the stairs. Ain't much, but the rest are taken."

"That's fine," said Charles, "as long as the water is hot."

"Laddie will heat it for you special, but it'll cost you extra. Supper is served at 6:30 in the dining room. Don't be late."

Charles nodded as he carefully penned his name: C. E. Bolton.

The next morning was wet, but Charles found himself almost giddy over the anticipation of his second hold up. He was finding it easier to dismiss the immoral aspects of his conduct, judging that Wells, Fargo & Company had no doubt stolen hundreds from a men all over the gold fields.

Charles headed out before daybreak. He'd chosen his spot well, ten miles from San Juan and a few miles above Smartsville. Talk was that the stage driver, Mike Hogan, had already been stopped two weeks earlier on the same stretch of road. With luck, he'd not be expecting another holdup. Apparently the man wasn't as smart as he could be.

When the coach came into sight, Charles felt a rush of excitement. As he had the first time around, he'd shoved a half dozen long sticks into the heavy brush, giving the illusion that gun barrels protruded at intervals along the trail.

The driver was on the box, but his attention had been diverted by one of the passengers who was shouting at him from below.

Charles stepped forward. This was his chance. "Halt, and throw down the box!" With his heart racing, he raised the barrel of his sawed-off shotgun. "Make it quick, now," he added for good measure. He wanted to smile at his own arrogance.

Mike Hogan—his jowls a wash of red and pink, accentuated by heavy orange-red brows and bright blue eyes—threw down the express box angrily. "You'll not get away with this," he growled, his Irish accent thick and harsh. "There'll be the devil to pay."

The horses stamped their impatience as Charles waved the coach on. "Perhaps, but not today, my good man. Not today!"

Charles watched until the stage had rattled away, then he attacked the iron box with savage energy.

Charles refolded the <u>Chronicle</u> and lay it on the table in front of him. What a grand twist: Hogan, in company with a posse of a dozen men, had returned to the scene in order to retrace the road agent's steps. Convinced that a gang of thieves had attacked him, the posse arrested five Spaniards, two Greeks, and an American.

The Spaniards and the Greeks would be easy stand-ins. Most likely, none of them spoke English, which gave Charles even more insurance against detection.

CHAPTER 46

Charles didn't find it necessary to leave the city again until late May. Telling his landlady that he'd be gone no less than a week, he carefully packed his valise, slipping his flour sack mask inside the shirtwaist his landlady had pressed and folded in thirds.

The steamboat to Marysville was filled with more cargo than with passengers, but Charles enjoyed the slower, gentler pace of the riverboats and side-wheelers. The world and its contrariness seemed to fall away as he strolled the upper decks and studied the river's changing landscape.

A shrill whistle startled him. Looking up, he realized Marysville was coming into view, and the port, in all its busyness, unfolded before him.

Disembarking, Charles headed to the hotel where he'd stayed in December. The cook there put out a fine meal, and suddenly he wanted to lose himself in a sizeable steak and a pint of cold ale.

"You heading to Sonora?" asked the loose-lipped tavern-keep.

Charles had asked for a simple, late supper, but the flabby, barrel-chested cook had taken the liberty of adding himself to the menu. He sat opposite Charles, eyeing him as he reached for a hunk of dark bread.

"I haven't decided yet, Friend," Charles said, trying hard to ignore the man's despicable manners. "I'm a newcomer," he added quickly. To himself, he added, "For certain I shall not return this a-way."

"Well, I hear tell that gold's gettin' harder to come by than a good woman."

"Indeed," returned Charles. He'd had about all of this fellow's conversation that he could manage. Folding his napkin, he excused himself.

The trail into the northern mines proved an easier trek than Charles had imagined, although he had never imagined such rugged peaks to rise up out of the valley's floor. He found a ride with two men headed up to the upper Klamath River, some 200 miles to the north. Their rig was hardly more than a cart pulled by two ancient mules, but they generously shared what food they had, declaring that it served a man well to keep to his Christian ways, even in they was in a god-forsaken land such as California.

"You been up into Oregon?" asked the older of the two men. He was a tall, gray-haired man with eyes the color of pea soup.

Charles shook his head. "Not yet. What's it like?"

The second man shrugged. Though younger and decidedly more rugged in stature, Charles thought he seemed less robust. He rode much of the time and sat, hunched over, wheezing nosily. Very likely he'd spent a lot of years bent over pick and shovel. "You got to be a farmer to really appreciate Oregon's valleys," he said. "Me, I'll take the mountains. From here all the way to the ocean, there's nothing but mountains and rivers and timber. Hudson Bay trappers, they combed the northern country for a time. Would've liked to have been a trapper myself," he added, "but I got the rheum and my bones don't take the cold for long. Besides, there's nothing left to trap anymore, 'cept a few stray Indians."

His partner laughed. "And you can't get much for their hides these days."

When the trio reached the northern mining settlement of

Hawkinsville, Charles bade his companions farewell. "I think I'll try my luck here," he said when they pressed him to go further. "My hands are itching," he added.

The older, taller man nodded. "My hands are itching', too. That's a good sign."

"Take care, Charles," returned the younger man. "And don't let your pocketbook out of sight. Me and my partner have seen at least a dozen men robbed for little more than a few grains of dust. Men falling on desperate times will take your last penny."

"Yes, well, thank you again, gentlemen," said Charles. He tapped the brim of his hat with the curve of his walking cane. "I do appreciate the advice, in addition to your generosity."

He watched as the rickety cart and weak-kneed mules clattered on up the trail.

Picking up his valise, Charles took an appraising glance around.

There were dozens of shacks and lean-tos lining the narrow street of the would-be town, but most were shabbily constructed. A few men, most as ragged as their shelters, sat on stools made of stumps, watching him. A couple women, also poorly dressed, peered out of shadowy doorways.

No doubt most of the townsfolk worked for bigger mining companies. He'd heard that a number of hard rock companies had taken over the smaller, less profitable mines.

He walked past the ramshackle community. This was no place to settle.

CHAPTER 47

Charles hiked up to the edge of a hill, to a spot where the road turned. He had been traversing the hilly terrain all day, and this was what he'd been looking for. Panting, he studied the location from both directions. The hillside was not steep but thickly dappled with brush and a few scattered trees, and a good driver would be concentrating on negotiating the grade, especially in the moonlight.

He looked around one more time. Yes, this was as good a place as any to stop the Roseburg to Yreka Stage.

Charles positioned himself behind a tree and alongside a rocky ledge that ran parallel to the road. Then he removed his mask and linen duster from the brown sack he'd stowed in his valise.

A short time later he heard the soft pounding of horses' hoofs and his heart began to pound in eerie synchronization.

Charles stepped into the trail when he spotted the approaching lights of the stage's hanging lamps. Waving one arm above his head, he hollered, "Whoa! Whoa!"

The driver instantly slowed the team, but even in the darkness, Charles could see his angry expression. A hard frown creased the shadowed contours of his rugged face. This was a man not easily buffaloed.

"Throw down the box!" Charles demanded and pressed the butt of his shotgun deeper into his shoulder. He didn't like the fact that the man's narrowed gaze had settled on him unflinchingly.

"You don't want to hold us up," hollered the Jehu. "The box ain't worth taking."

Charles swung the barrel of his gun in a circle. "I'm not asking," he hollered back. Then he took a quick breath and glanced over his shoulder as if looking for reinforcements. "Fellas, if he don't throw the box down, take steady aim, you hear?" He carefully raised his eyes back up to the driver. "They'll make mincemeat out of you," he said as calmly as he could.

Again the driver stalled. "You're making a mistake. I only got supplies and a little mail."

"Do you want them to shoot you?" Charles took a step toward the restless team, trying hard to quell his own anxiety. "Do you want me to shoot you?"

He waited. What if the fool didn't listen? He hadn't even loaded his gun.

"Take the box," grumbled the driver, "but you ain't getting much for your trouble."

Charles' mouth was as dry as the ground beneath his feet. "It'll be enough."

Charles boarded Yreka's afternoon stage three days later. Donned in short coat and hat, with his walking stick in one hand and his valise in the other, he reckoned his companions would be surprised to know just who was joining them on the jaunt south.

The driver shouted his last order. "Toss that box up, Henry! I'm keepin' it bolted down, good and tight. And hand up that extra shotgun. No road agents are gonna take this box without takin' a bullet first."

Charles feigned interest in a pair of dogs that were fighting outside the open window.

A man sitting opposite pointed to the dogs. "I'd put money on the scrappy one. He's got the guts to go after a dog twice his size."

The man next to Charles nodded. "Talk about scrappy dogs. Did you hear about the holdup a few days ago? The Southbound stage got hit. A. C. Adams, the driver, tried to talk the fool out of it, sayin' he was only carryin' a few gold notes, but the thief wouldn't be deterred."

Charles stifled a smile. Contrary to the man's assumption, the booty he'd wrangled had been more than enough to keep him in style for a number of months. "I hadn't heard," he returned blandly. "Anyone hurt?"

"No. In fact, the bandit didn't even bother with the passengers. Didn't even notice there was any, I guess."

"That's good," returned Charles.

"Latest word is that the fool was caught, yesterday, I do believe. He was hitchin' a ride outside Canyonville, but it didn't take long for the teamster to figure out just who his acquaintance was. The sheriff of Douglas County nabbed him almost as soon as word crossed his desk."

"So, he headed into Oregon?" asked Charles. Smiling to himself, he let his head fall back against the rough boards of the mud wagon's interior.

CHAPTER 48

Special Agent James B. Hume pulled off his coat as Deputy Sheriff John Halleck led him into the front office of the new Yreka jail. "So, Halleck, I understand we have the thief. Where is he?"

Halleck smiled. "He's locked up. In there."

Hume nodded. "Let me see him."

Hume strode up to the jail cell, his gaze fixed on the man behind the bars. He was certainly not what he expected, that much was certain. This man was as thin and as nervous as a stray cat trapped in a room full of rocking chairs. His dark eyes flitted from Halleck to Hume.

"I ain't who they think I am, Mister," he said, stepping forward.

"No? Who do they think you are?" returned Hume. He'd heard enough to know the man must have a well-practiced alibi. "Why did they bring you in?"

"For that stage robbery," he said. "Only I ain't ever held up a stage. I guess I was traveling the same trail. That's all. I swear," he added breathlessly.

Hume glanced back at Halleck. "Did you examine his boots? I understand the thief left a singular track, with large nails and well-worn soles."

Halleck shook his head. "Nobody mentioned any such thing to me."

Hume turned to the man. "Let me have your boots."

He pointed to Halleck. "He took 'em."

Halleck nodded. "We got a nice new jail, you know.

I'd like to keep it that way."

Hume snorted and followed Halleck back to the front desk. The boots were sitting neatly paired beside the wood stove.

He picked them up and walked back to the jail cell. "These yours?"

The man behind the bars nodded.

Frowning, Hume handed them back to Halleck. "Let him go, Deputy. You got the wrong man."

"Yeah? How can you tell all that from a lousy pair of old boots?"

Hume resisted the urge to call the man the idiot he seemed to be. "We've tracked this man before, remember?"

It wasn't hard to lose oneself or fabricate a new identity in San Francisco. For that, Charles was grateful. He thoroughly enjoyed his new role as mining engineer and looked forward to his visits to the police station and restaurants and bars that grew more fashionable each day. Still, his favorite place was the Palace Hotel.

Donning a newly starched shirt, which he'd picked up earlier from the laundry, Charles gathered up his linen duster, walking stick, and derby. The day was inordinately warm but he had a long distance to travel before he could rest.

The ferry to Petaluma was crowded. Women, walking arm and arm with gentlemen, and children, running to and fro, reminded him that California was becoming a civilized place. No longer just dirty miners and rowdy drifters, but whole families now traveled together.

Charles sat down near the railing and watched the parade of travelers moving past him. It was the little girls who most caught his eye. With ribbons flying from their bonnets like pink and white kite tails, he couldn't help but wonder as to the health and well-being of his own daughters. It'd been several years since he'd even attempted to write them. Of course, Mary Elizabeth no doubt cursed the ground he slept on these days.

But who could blame her?

He shook himself. Yes, if life could be relived, he might choose to do things differently. But regret was senseless and painful and didn't serve a man well.

Besides, he'd made his choices. Like his mother often said, "You got to pay the fiddler if you want to dance."

CHAPTER 49

"Excuse me."

Startled, Charles looked up from his newspaper, then scrambled to his feet. The woman standing in front of him smiled brightly. "I'm sorry, do we know one another?"

"Indeed. We met once, I believe?" Extending her fan, she pointed to the seat nearest his. "May I?"

"Forgive me. Please, sit down." He glanced around the hotel dining room to see if she'd abandoned a companion, but no one seemed to be waiting in the foyer or in the nearly-empty room.

The woman eased into the cane chair, her full skirts spilling out over the scalloped edges of the seat. Wrapping her gloved hands around the handle of her lace fan, she smiled again. "We met years ago," she repeated, raising a brow. "I was serving tables in Marysville. I recall you came in with Mr. Beckwourth."

Charles dropped into his own chair and turned, his heart beating soundly as he studied the well-groomed and lovely creature now speaking. "Jim? I haven't seen him since— well, since then. I hope my manners kept me in good stead, Miss—?"

She smiled. "Yes, absolutely. And the name is Mary. Mary Vollmer."

"At your service. I'm Charles Bolton. Most recently from San Francisco, but originally from New York."

"New York City?"

"No, Plessis, a small place along the St. Lawrence

River."

She nodded. "Well, I have also settled far from my roots, but I love adventure. Right now I live outside Oroville. I live and work at the Woodville Hotel."

"I've stayed there," returned Charles, "once or twice."

"I hope to see you again, then, Mr. Bolton."

"You can be sure of it," returned Charles. His eyes could not break away from the curve of Mary Vollmer's cheek. "My business takes me to the gold fields quite often."

Charles arrived at the Woodville two weeks later. The thought of Mary had not left him since their chance meeting in San Francisco, and for the first time in more years than he cared to admit, he *felt* something warm moving through his bones.

He scarcely called it love. Perhaps infatuation, but, nonetheless, it made the world around him glisten, as if everything had been doused in sunshine.

Hopefully he'd not imagined her interest.

But her smile was genuine and her eyes reflected her pleasure. "Mr. Bolton. Please, come in. I certainly didn't expect you—"

"No?"

"Well, I didn't expect you today." She ushered him into the parlor. "I'm afraid I've got some work to do in the kitchen."

"I don't mind," he said, then followed her to the kitchen where she'd obviously been preparing lunch. There was a slab of bacon, a bowl of peeled potatoes, and several fresh loaves of bread. The aroma of roasted chicken filled the room. "Smells good."

Mary flushed. "Feeding hungry men is what we do best. Unfortunately, Sadie and Ella, who normally work in the kitchen, aren't here. Sadie asked if I'd take over; she's soft on one of the miners, and Ella is ill. But dinner is almost ready."

"Perhaps I should come another day?"

Mary shook the hair that had fallen across her cheek out of her eyes. She shook her head. "Don't go. There will be plenty."

"I can pay."

"Yes, well, that goes without saying." She smiled and Charles laughed.

There was something wonderfully unpredictable about Mary, and whatever it was, it was bewitching.

"Not that I'd charge you myself, but Cookie counts every penny and double-checks every ledger."

"As I said, I can pay. I wouldn't want anyone to think I was less than honest."

"Very well," returned Mary. "Why don't you take those plates over there into the dining room. There should be eight. Oh, and those knives, as well. I'll finish the applesauce and then start the potatoes to boil."

Charles smiled. "My mother would be proud to see me at work in the kitchen. I don't think I ever did more than carry water for her when I was young."

"Surely you helped occasionally?"

"No, not. My father never stepped foot into the kitchen and he disavowed any son who didn't follow his lead. Of course, I often sneaked in to steal a freshly-baked molasses cookie or hunk of bread. Mother was a splendid cook."

Mary laughed and the sound of her infectious laughter pleased him. "Well, that's something then," she said and returned to her work. "I expect anyone who steps into this kitchen to lend a hand, not just steal a bite."

Charles crossed over to a small wooden table that leaned against one wall of the kitchen and picked up eight ironstone plates and a handful of knives. The remaining wooden utensils, bowls, and dusting of flour over all reminded him of his mother's kitchen. She rarely left a dish

166

unturned or a surface area clean when she was cooking.

The sudden memory of his mother was like a pin prick. He'd not thought of her or anyone in days, perhaps weeks. Indeed, he'd grown so used to thinking only of himself, it was a surprise to discover he actually missed someone from his past.

"There!" Mary broke into his thoughts. "If you would, take a seat in the dining room. I'll ring the bell. And whatever you do, do not sit near Ben. He'll be wearing red suspenders, and he'll talk your ear off if you give him half a chance."

Again Charles smiled. He liked Mary's directness. "I'll take heed," he said, and followed her into the next room.

She's a woman with grit, he thought suddenly.

A woman for me.

CHAPTER 50

Mary seemed as content with their developing relationship as did Charles, their time together filled with fine food and laughter. He bought lavish gifts when he could, even sent away for fabrics and notions, for Mary was as adept with needle and thread as any woman he'd ever known. She appreciated even the smallest remembrances.

Of course, he had not yet revealed anything of his alter ego, letting her think only that he was a mining engineer with several successful claims under his belt. The lie didn't sit well, and, for a time he wondered if he shouldn't return to mining. Simply stop.

Unfortunately, he'd never been much good at anything except soldiering or holding up stages. And he could never afford the extravagant doo-dads he brought Mary if he returned to the world of honest pay. No, there was nothing he could do but keep his profession a secret. At least for now.

He did try gambling on a more regular basis, but before long, his winning turned to losing and he abandoned the effort. It seemed he'd lost his poker face.

Well, perhaps he could stretch the remaining money he'd stashed in his room back in San Francisco.

As the months passed, however, his small cache was gone. That left him no alternative but to locate a new source of revenue.

Packing lightly, he headed back to San Francisco, then north, to Sonoma County. Almost hoping he would feel some sort of remorse, the old excitement returned.

Charles glanced at his watch. Not even 11:00 yet, the August morning sun burned through the fabric of his shirt and duster.

Looking up and down the steep track, he knew he'd selected a good spot, just past the curve at the top of Myers Grade, four miles from the old Russian fort and even further from James Henry's Hotel and Stage Stop. Duncan Mills was the next stop on the route, but there would be ample time to scurry away before the driver could rally a posse.

He stepped out into the road when he heard the approaching sounds of the stage. He leveled his gun and took a slow, steadying breath. Almost simultaneously, the driver spotted him and drew the team to a complete stop.

One of the passengers leaned out of the window but, catching sight of Charles, drew back, horrified.

"Throw the box down, Mister. And don't give me reason to shoot." Charles kept his shotgun aimed at the belly of the driver. "That goes for those inside the coach, too."

"You're a fool," returned the Jehu boldly. "Wells, Fargo and Company ain't takin' kindly to being held up any more. There'll be a posse directly."

"Don't be offering advice," said Charles. "Just do as I say and no one will get hurt. I don't relish putting a bullet between anyone's eyes, but I assure you, I can do it. "

As the box fell to the ground, Charles called out, "Now, turn around, carefully."

The driver reluctantly complied, turning away so that he could not see Charles hammer at the lock with the axe he'd stowed close at hand. Neither did he see Charles remove the two sacks of mail and coin, replacing them with a waybill across which were scrawled several lines of verse. "Let them mull this over," he mumbled to himself.

When all was accomplished, Charles stepped forward and slapped the rear of the lead horse. "All right, get moving! And don't think about anything but getting out of here."

The driver hollered at the team and drove on, his glance back a quick, bitter one.

Charles tapped the brim of his hat. It wouldn't do to appear unnerved. Then he headed into the brush.

With the money tucked into his vest pocket, and a check made out to Fisk Brothers folded inside the brim of his hat, Charles knew he had to get to Healdsburg as quickly as possible. No doubt a posse would be on his trail before nightfall.

But time was on his side. At least for the present.

CHAPTER 51

Though surprised, Mary was pleased to see him.

Dressed in a striped cotton dress and apron, with no adornment, Charles found her amazingly beautiful. Her braided hair lay coiled against the nape of her neck and her brown eyes sparkled under well-arched brows.

"Oh, Charles, you're a day early," she scolded. She led the way into the large front parlor of the Woodville. "Have a seat, please, while I finish up in the kitchen. Ella is being rather cantankerous, and Sadie is nowhere in sight. I believe she's run off with her miner, at long last. But you'd think there had been a colossal strike or bank robbery with all the traffic moving through here today."

Charles chuckled. "No need to apologize. I finished my business early and decided to surprise you. I'll wait in the saloon."

Mary smiled. "That might be best. I do find you a terrible distraction, Mr. Bolton."

Later they sat under the moonlit sky, Charles smoking a thin cigar he'd purchased after their meal.

"I didn't know you smoked," Mary said, her gaze following the trail of smoke.

"Not often," he said. "Only when I'm in, say, a contemplative mood."

"Oh?" She studied his profile, wondering what he might be pondering.

"A habit my father engaged in, actually," he said, as if surprised. "Whenever we saw him with a cheroot we knew something was working on him. Unfortunately, the consequences of that serious thinking resulted in—well, it doesn't matter now," he added, more to himself than aloud.

"Your father was a serious man?" Mary's curiosity was piqued for it wasn't often Charles offered her a glimpse into his past.

"Much too serious, while David and I were not serious enough."

He'd mentioned David so often that Mary knew he'd been his favorite brother. The little he'd spoken of his death, however, revealed how heavily it still weighed on him. All in all, she rarely asked him questions about his life, though she very much desired to know more.

Charles sighed. "You're not going to ask what I'm brooding over?" He raised his brows and smiled.

Mary felt a sudden heat pass through her. Of course she was curious about this 'contemplative' mood. But more than that, she was suddenly nervous. The last year in Charles' company had given her such joy she was afraid to speak of it for fear it would dissipate like the smoke of his cheroot into the night air. She feigned indifference. "Not so curious. Don't they say that food for thought can oftimes bring on indigestion?"

Charles laughed. "Well, I'm bound to tell you anyway, for there will be no secrets between us. That much I've decided."

"I've certainly told you everything of consequence in my life."

He reached for her fingers. "I know. You have been far more honest than anyone I've ever known. And for many reasons, I don't have a right to ask more of you," he said, "but I must."

She waited, her heartbeat filling her head with soft thumps.

"You know I shall never ask Mary Elizabeth for a

divorce. If only for the girls' sake."

She sighed. They'd been over this several times. "Yes, Charles. And I'll never ask you to divorce her. Marriage was hardly an arrangement I found tolerable in my own life." She'd already told him of the useless man she'd married and followed out to California. He died after losing every penny they had saved.

"But I would, if I could, marry you," broke in Charles. "Do you understand that? Marriage to you is an arrangement I would find highly desirable."

Mary shrugged. It wasn't likely she'd have occasion to know the depth of his declaration. Irritated, she replied curtly, "Is that what you wanted to tell me?"

He wrapped his fingers around hers and drew her closer. "That's only part of want I need to tell you. There's more. Much more. But first you must promise that what I tell you will not alter how you feel. I don't think I could stand that. And it's taken me months to realize that I must, after all, tell you everything."

She took a deep breath, wondering if she might choke on the fear welling up inside her. "Nothing, nothing, you could say or do would change the way I feel. You are stuck with me, Charles. I'd follow you to the ends of the earth if that's what you asked me to do."

"Well," returned Charles, smiling. "I won't ask you to do that. Not unless it becomes absolutely necessary." He drew his hands out from under hers, then took her slender fingers and placed them against the wall of his chest. She could feel the pounding of his heart against them even as the heat of his flesh burned through the homespun shirt he wore.

He leaned forward and whispered into her ear, "I cannot live without you, Mary. Not now. Not ever."

His next words sent another kind of shiver down her spine. "But I'm not who you think I am, and you may find the truth difficult to bear."

CHAPTER 52

The headlines were everywhere: "Highwayman Leaves Behind Mysterious Message!" And "Black Bart: The Elusive Highwayman!"

Charles refolded the Chronicle and smiled. He hadn't thought about how the flimsy bit of verse he'd left behind would titillate and torment the Wells, Fargo & Company's detectives or the detail-seeking journalists, but the results of his spontaneity had been too tantalizing not to enjoy. There wasn't a newspaper from Yreka to Monterey that wasn't now making predictions as to when and where the notorious gentleman bandit would next appear.

The man sitting opposite Charles chuckled. A member of the San Francisco police force, Officer Blackwell often stopped to visit with Charles over breakfast at the New York Restaurant.

He pointed to the article. "Listen to what the fool wrote," he said and cleared his throat. "'I've labored long and hard for bread, for honor and for riches. But on my corns too long you've tread, you fine-haired sons of bitches.'" He chuckled again. "Still, a clever thief is still a thief, and this road agent has Wells, Fargo & Company detectives steaming, especially Hume." He shook his head soberly. "No doubt they will trip him up soon enough."

"Indeed," remarked Charles.

"Oh, yes," returned Blackwell. "There's an $800 reward out now. That should soften someone's conscience."

"Hmm," said Charles.

"But he's making a fool of them all until then," continued the officer, "and Hume don't relish playing the fool. Lord knows I'd never want to tangle with the man. He's got steel in his veins and sand in his gut."

Charles listened. He liked this James Hume, and he'd listened to all the descriptions of him with relish. Every story revealed the man's nerve and dedication, making him a worthy adversary and Wells, Fargo & Company a more enticing target. Indeed, if he hadn't been the focus of Hume's search, he'd welcome getting to know the man personally.

Charles glanced at his pocket watch. "I have an appointment, Blackwell," he said. He rose and extended his right hand. "If I don't see you for a few days, I'll see you when I return."

"I do believe you must bring in a fortune with those mines, Bolton, but you keep more to yourself than men with half your coin."

Charles laughed. "I rarely miss an opportunity to keep quiet. You never know when someone might decide to relieve you of your purse."

"Ah," said Blackwell, "very true. I'm often more forthright than prudent."

As Charles left the New York Restaurant, he smiled. His ruse was working well. For the most part, he had become a well-respected gentleman and counted among his friends many of San Francisco's finest citizens. His life had truly taken an upward turn.

Most importantly, he'd found love at last. Even his confession, days before his last robbery, had not dulled Mary's responses to him; in fact, he suspected she found his secret identity exciting, for she had clung to him and kissed him ardently before letting him go.

Still, it was a relief to have lifted the veil of deceit that had hung between them. No longer did he have to lie about his travels or absences. No longer did he have to fabricate the stories of how he made his living. She loved him without reservation, something he'd never experienced with Mary Elizabeth, even with the hallowed tethers of marriage and family binding them together.

CHAPTER 53

He found it unnecessary to hold up another stage for almost a year. Living off what he'd taken in the last two robberies, and actually winning a few substantial hands at the faro table, he resisted the urge to take up costume or gun for as long as he could.

Unfortunately, the money finally petered out, and Charles knew he'd have to locate a new opportunity. So, on July 25, 1878, he robbed the Quincy to Oroville stage, and unloaded more than $600 worth of valuables.

He'd liked to have made more on the deal.

Later, after he returned to Woodville under the cover of night, Mary showed him the newspaper clipping detailing the holdup. He folded it and dropped it into the pocket of her apron.

"Tomorrow we'll have time to talk. Right now I could use a pint of ale and maybe a beef steak."

"I have some cold tongue."

"Perfect."

The next day, Charles and Mary walked down to the spring, which lay a quarter mile away from the hotel.

Charles shook out a blanket. Mary, dropping to her knees, opened the small picnic basket she'd packed earlier. She handed Charles a chunk of cheese and a thick slice of bread.

"Listen," she said and pulled the newspaper clipping out of her pocket. "They really don't know much about you, do they? It says, 'The stage from Quincy to Oroville was stopped on Thursday afternoon, about a mile above Berry Creek, by a masked highwayman, and WF & Co.'s express box was taken. Three passengers were aboard, but were unharmed. The stage proceeded to Berry Creek, where a gun was procured and two of the passengers returned to the scene of the crime, but could find no trace of the robber or the box. It was thought that there was little coin, if any, in the box.'"

Mary glanced at the diamond ring on Charles' finger. "Too bad they don't have all the facts."

Charles smiled and she laughed.

"I especially like the verse," she said, then read on. "'Here I lay me down to sleep, to wait the coming morrow. Perhaps success, perhaps defeat, and everlasting sorrow. Let come what will, I'll try it on, my condition can't be worse, but if there's money in the box, it's munny in my purse.' Whatever possessed you to leave another poem behind, Charles? Don't you think it might provide a clue to your identity?"

"Actually, I've come to a new philosophy in the last year," he returned, shrugging. "If it's a fool I am, why then, I'll be a dandy."

Mary couldn't resist his humor, his odd way of looking at the world. It wasn't just refreshing; it felt right somehow. Like Charles, she'd been a rebel all her life, and had even wondered if she'd ever find a man who could appreciate her outspokenness. "You are a wild one, Charles Bowles." She drew out his last name carefully; he'd finally given up that lie on their last visit. "But I should add that you better be a bit more careful. You are not beyond being discovered eventually. Woodville is a popular stopping place for miners, loggers, and detectives."

Charles drew her to him, pushing aside his plate of food. "I'll be as careful as a naked man climbing a barbed wire fence, okay?"

He kissed away her laughter.

178

Charles' next target was an easy one, and staying at the Woodville provided the perfect alibi. No one would suspect his staying extra days in Mary's company out of the ordinary, and the fact that it would be a mere five days after his last holdup would take Wells, Fargo & Company thoroughly by surprise.

It was a cool July 30 morning when Charles settled himself behind a tree just opposite a tight elbow turn on the LaPorte to Oroville road. Placing his tools and gear alongside him, he listened for the familiar sound of the approaching team. Though this would be his sixth official stage robbery, the sound of horses' thundering toward him was still a stout elixir, leaving his nerves raw, his heart pounding.

When the stage slowed to negotiate the turn, Charles stepped out in front of the lead horse. "Hands up and throw down the box and mail bag," he called. "Come on! You know what I want."

The driver, later identified as Dan Barry, slowed the animals. It was clear he recognized the bandit. "You won't get away with this," he said. "Your days are numbered."

From inside the coach, a female passenger gasped.

Charles, his attention still on the driver, called out, "Don't worry, ma'am. I won't bother you. I'll be through in a minute and then you'll be on your way." To the driver he said, "Sit still and you'll live to a ripe old age."

Charles broke open the express box and smiled. More than $100 in gold, as well as a silver watch, had been tucked inside.

He tipped his hat as he motioned for the stage driver to press on. Grumbling, the driver cast him an angry glance.

Charles stepped aside. "Thank you. 'Twas well worth my time, after all!" he called after the disappearing coach.

CHAPTER 54

Charles entered the parlor at the Woodville, relieved no one was in sight. He hung his coat neatly on the peg near the door and set his hat on the shelf above it, then dusted himself off carefully. He settled into a chair that overlooked the veranda and folded his hands primly. Another patron Charles had met on prior trips wandered in a few minutes later.

"Ah, Charles," he said. "I was hoping you hadn't left. The boys are starting up a little game in the saloon. Thought you might like to join us."

Charles smiled. "Why, George, I was thinking that perhaps everyone had disappeared on me. I'd relish a chance to win back my last one hundred dollars."

George grinned. "It's not often any of us get the edge on you."

"Not so, I warrant. But, a sharp eye is the mother of good luck, George, and I think yours was sharper last time than mine."

Charles dreaded leaving for San Francisco, because leaving Mary was becoming more and more difficult. In her presence he felt satisfied and wanted little more than to be with her. He suspected she disliked his leaving as much as he did, but she was stubbornly independent and insisted he go, the sooner the better. "You can't stay here," she whispered at breakfast the next morning. "They may yet begin to trace your retreat, and I couldn't bare it if you were caught, Charles. I used to find your enterprises titillating, but more and more I find your work nerve-wracking."

"Mary," soothed Charles, "I've always been one to play a hand close to my chest. I won't take unnecessary chances."

Even still, he boarded the afternoon train and headed back to the harbor city.

Charles later heard that a ragged tramp had been arrested for his crime after the townsfolk demanded some action be taken, but was then released for lack of evidence. Robberies in the region were becoming far too frequent, however, and Wells, Fargo & Company was suffering sorely from the losses.

By the end of September, it became clear to Charles that he needed to unload another treasure box. Rather than returning to the LaPorte area, even though he'd have quick access to Mary, he headed to Mendocino County. On Wednesday evening, October 2, he settled himself beside a large boulder along Forsythe Creek on the Cloverdale to Arcata stage route. The spot offered a view of the road for a mile in either direction.

He removed an apple from his pocket and let his head drop back against his stony fortress. He'd tramped long and hard to get here and he was tired, but his mask, sawed-off shotgun and axe were within easy reach, so he gave himself up to dreaming of Mary.

At the sound of the approaching team, he threw down his half-finished apple. Donning his mask, he grabbed his gun and jumped to his feet.

The team was slowing down in order to make the tight curve, and the delay gave Charles the opportunity to call out to the driver. He raised his gun. "Throw down the box!"

The Jehu, clearly angry, was unable to grab his own shotgun in time to protect himself and his express box. Instead he brought the team to a halt and sighing, wrestled the box out himself. "You were clever, that's for sure," he grumbled.

"The mail sack, too," Charles hollered.

Frowning, the driver threw the mailbag into the dirt a few feet from Charles.

Charles nodded. "Okay, now drive like hell!"

In minutes the stage had thundered away and Charles, taking up his axe, broke into the treasure box. He frowned when he realized he'd captured less than $50 for his trouble.

"Hardly worth the trouble," he said half-aloud, then realized it wouldn't be long before deputies were on their way. He shouldered his bedroll and equipment and headed into the brush.

Frustrated by the amount he'd tendered, Charles traveled east. Darkness overtook him, but he kept moving. He refused to return home with such a paltry sum.

But he was hungry and needed a good meal. He'd find an inn or perhaps put up at a miner's cabin. Round these parts people were not adverse to helping out a stranger. He'd met some fine folks in his wanderings.

On Thursday, October 3, he held up the stage between Covelo and Ukiah, a few miles north of Centerville. After that he moved quickly, covering more than 70 miles in 48 hours.

No doubt detectives would be tracking him hard this time. He had pushed his luck and didn't want that luck to dry up.

At least not yet.

CHAPTER 55

"Charles, you better lay low."

Charles smiled down at Mary who was seated at his feet, head resting against his knees. He sighed. He'd never known such comfort in all of his life. He stroked her hair. "I don't need to be testing Fate for a spell," he whispered.

She snuggled closer. "Good. I worry when you're gone, and it seems you enjoy taking chances just a little too much."

"Not so much," he said. "Not so much anymore." He tickled the edge of her ear and she squirmed.

Charles was true to his word. Traveling back and forth from San Francisco to Woodville, he lived modestly and when necessary, did a little gambling. He even took a job mining, joining a couple of different crews at a few hard rock mines around in the region. But the work was harder than he liked and the conditions deplorable. He knew he'd grown soft. Still it gave him access to Mary and to bits of interesting information.

Winter time was a time of waiting and he and Mary spent long evenings together, either in the parlor of the hotel, or out walking. They talked about nothing in particular, but about everything at the same time. It was an amazing thing to him, since he and Mary Elizabeth had found less and less to talk about while they were married, unless it was about the girls. Mary was different, and he'd known it from the first moment they met.

Still, there were the girls. His girls. His only children.

The idea that he might never see his three beautiful

daughters again in this life suddenly sobered him, even though he tried to avoid thinking about them most of the time.

But alone or on occasion, he couldn't help himself. He wondered where they were and what they were doing. No doubt they thought little of him, or dismissed him as a ne'er do well, but well they should. He'd abandoned them, along with Mary Elizabeth. He should have at least sent them money along the way.

Perhaps his father had been right. He was no good. He brought disappointment to those who loved him.

"You're quiet tonight, Charles," whispered Mary. She moved nearer the fire, which roared in the enormous fireplace, one hand on her hip and one hand on the mantel. Her form was reflected in the shadows that danced along the wall behind her.

"Yes, far too quiet," he admitted. He took a long sip of tea, though it had gone cold. "Do you think, Mary, that a man can ever be forgiven such despicable disregard of his children?"

Mary sighed. He'd asked her this question in as many ways as it was possible for a man to ask. She nodded, resisting the urge to rush to him and throw her arms around him. "Charles, you are a decent man. Not altogether honest, of course, but a decent man. You'd never hurt man, woman, or child intentionally. And you left your wife and girls to find a better life. Mayhap you've given them a better life by leaving them. You weren't happy, and I don't think Mary Elizabeth or the girls would have been happy with the way life had deteriorated, either."

Charles seemed to listen, but Mary knew it did little to assuage the guilt he felt. They'd had this conversation so often it was difficult to wade through it again, but she did so. He needed her to, and she knew she'd do whatever it took to make him happy. For in truth, she didn't believe Charles was a happy man. He harbored too many doubts, too many feelings, and they seemed to torment him, especially on long, dark winter nights.

"Come here," said Charles.

Mary sat and snuggled close.

"Whatever would I do without you?" he whispered.

By early summer, however, Charles felt an itch that he knew he'd have to scratch—sooner or later. Taking stock of his resources, he turned his attention once more on the region surrounding Woodville. There were many stage routes and if he kept to a rigorous schedule and chose wisely, he'd be able to back-track to Mary without ruffling any suspicions.

On June 21, 1879, Charles held up the stage on the Forbestown-Oroville Road, just three miles west of Forbestown. Unfortunately what he recovered from the express box and the mail pouches was not as rich as he'd supposed. Forbestown was such an industrious town, he'd imagined his take would be substantial. Still, he beat feet back to Woodville and Mary.

"It won't keep me for long," he confided in Mary later that night. He'd arrived well after midnight and she'd hid him in the basement below the kitchen till morning.

"Oh, Charles, please, wait it out," pleaded Mary. "The men talked of nothing else at supper. News is that Hume, the Wells, Fargo & Company detective, will be scouring every stage route and state hostelry around the mines."

Charles shrugged. "He has nothing that will lead him to me. I left no clues."

"Maybe not, but he's not a man to fool with," Mary said. "They say he's as keen as a coon on a track, and he's determined to catch the man that now dogs him. And some swear he's got you half-figured out already."

Charles pondered the likelihood that Hume could know more than anyone else. Certainly he had little to go on, at this point.

Still, he promised Mary he'd wait a while before taking on another job.

But by late October, he was as restless as ever. After a heated discussion with Mary, he headed north, to Shasta County. There he spent a night at a small inn, where he learned that the night stage would soon be coming through. The driver, Jim Smithson, was well-known and well-liked, and the lively conversation about the man's high-falutin' airs intrigued Charles. A good whip was a man worth his salt.

On October 25, between Bass Station and Buckeye, Charles held up the Roseburg, Oregon-Yreka-Redding stage, but he took no chances as he ordered Smithson to drop the express box and the mailbags. The man had the sharp eye of a marksman.

"It's been a pleasure," said Charles after fanning the stage past.

Mr. Smithson turned and stared him down, his long pencil nose and furrowed brows a reminder that this man would not long forget Charles' assault.

Two days later, Charles went on to hold up the Alturas to Redding stage. Perhaps two robberies, back to back, would put him ahead just enough that he might spend a year or two out of the loop and out of the honorable Wells, Fargo & Company detective's path.

CHAPTER 56

In 1880, Charles robbed a series of stages, the first in Sonoma County, on the Point Arena-Duncan Mills Road and the second on the Weaverville to Redding Road on Trinity Mountain, not far from Last Chance Station. It was a warm September day.

This holdup proved more difficult than Charles anticipated. In addition to the Wells Fargo express box and mailbags, there was an iron box attached to the stage.

"Get down," he ordered the driver, "and move aside."

The driver climbed down from the stage, but refused to move away. Charles, keeping his shotgun pointed at the man, turned and tried to hack at the locked box.

"You ain't gonna get in there," said the Jehu.

Charles didn't respond except to hack more furiously at the iron hinges and lock. At last, frustrated and growing nervous, he circled the barrel of his gun in the face of the driver. "Get on up there," he ordered, "and don't look back."

He thought he heard the driver laugh as the stage pulled away, the iron box still fastened securely to the side of the coach. In all, he'd netted little more than a hundred dollars, not enough to satisfy him, but enough that he'd take what he got.

At least for the moment. At least until he figured out where he might go next.

Determined to set to rights his reputation as the best stage thief, he headed further north. He did not return to Woodville or San Francisco, but continued on through Siskiyou County and into Jackson County, Oregon. The region was more rugged, and if he waited for a nighttime stage, perhaps just north of the Oregon-California state line, he might do very well.

He settled himself along the Roseburg, Oregon-Yreka-California Road, and after all was said and done, Charles was pleased. He counted out more than a thousand dollars from the Wells, Fargo & Company's treasure box.

He entered the stage stop at Henley late the next day, his tools and satchel well hidden in the brush some miles off the trail. Brushing off the road dust, he smiled at the woman who stood behind the counter.

"Welcome," she said, her gaze taking in Charles' relatively expensive coat and walking stick. He'd learned that appearances were not only deceiving, but they made his approach and retreats relatively simple.

"Hello," he said, smiling broadly. "Ale, please, and a meal?"

"Of course, of course," returned the woman. "I've also some apple cobbler, if you've got a sweet tooth."

"Madam," said Charles, "I have not had a good cobbler in a month of Sundays. Tell me, when will the next stage be coming through? My poor bones have taken enough of a beating for a day or two."

Buoyed by his recent round of successful holdups, Charles refused to return south until he'd filled his pockets to overflowing. No doubt Mary would be pacing the floor, determined that he'd end up in jail, but the temptation to locate another rich take, spurred him to stay in the area.

He took up a menial job working for a small crew of miners, but kept to himself, biding his time till word of a good haul came along.

A week later, he found the opportunity. The clerks at the Henley Stop were easily plied for information and so, on September 23, Charles excused himself from breakfast, then headed north once more, into Jackson County, along the Roseburg-Oregon-Redding Road. This holdup proved as profitable as the last and Charles netted a thousand dollars in gold dust, in addition to the contents of the mail sacks.

The last holdup Charles attempted during 1880 was once more in Siskiyou County, on the Roseburg, Oregon-Redding Route, just a mile south of the Oregon-California line. It was nearly dark as Charles approached the stage and ordered the driver, Joe Mason, to halt.

Mason was furious and just as Charles demanded he throw down the box, the driver grabbed his own axe and swung it at Charles' head.

Stunned, Charles dropped to the ground and ran.

It was time to return to Mary.

CHAPTER 57

It was ten months before Charles held up another stage.

Mary, having grown more cautious, reminded Charles that he wasn't in the business of hurting anyone, but that this kind of business might well bring grief to people without intention. Such a notion didn't settle well with her.

He maintained that his holdups hurt no one but the great Wells, Fargo & Company. "They ply their trade to the detriment of the small-time businessman," he said.

Mary shook her head. "You are a stubborn man. Do you want to get caught?"

The two sat along a plank bench, just a short distance from the Woodville Hotel. Charles had arrived the evening before and Mary, always pleased to see him, frowned when he told her he was planning another holdup along the Jacksonville, Oregon, to Yreka, California, stage route.

"Please, Charles, you must reconsider. The money isn't that good. Seems you've come up dry a few times lately, and one of these days, you'll come up with a bullet right between the eyes instead of a little gold dust. It rattles me, I confess."

"Mary," said Charles. He laced one hand through hers and drew her fingers to his lips. "You must trust me. I know what I'm about. These stage drivers don't want to get hurt any more than I want to hurt them. In truth, most of them are half-outlaw and relish the thrill of pushing through to their destination while outwitting thieves like me. I don't doubt a few even hope a bandit will step into their path.

Everyone wants to be a hero at least once in his life."

Mary rolled her eyes. "I know better than that, dear Charles. There are drivers in and out of here every day. Believe me, if they could get their guns on you before you stepped out of the brush, they'd sooner send you to kingdom-come. They do not relish the blow you deal to their pride or the embarrassment of having to explain how you stole their booty right out from under them, especially when James Hume comes to town. He's determined to catch you, and there are posters finding their way into every tavern and way-station in the area. I just threw one out."

Charles shrugged. "Hume is obviously a good man, and I've heard that he's a devil for details. But my good luck has far from run out, Mary. You are proof of that."

Mary pushed him gently. "Are you sure? Continued good luck may be undeserved or may signal a certain carelessness."

"Nah. Besides, bad luck is often just as undeserved. Believe me, I have had my share of that over the years. I'm only making up for some of what was taken from me. Or, at least, that's how I see it."

Mary studied Charles closely. She knew he believed he'd been handed some bad hands over the years, but she didn't see how holding up Wells, Fargo, & Company could square it. "You're playing with fire, Charles. I tell you, this Hume is doggedly going after every bit of evidence. He's made it his business to ask all manner of questions about you, and folks are eager to help him. He's quite convincing."

"And I've met more than a few people in my travels who, I suspect, know what I'm about, and they don't seem too disturbed over it. After all, Wells, Fargo & Company takes a good cut of the gold that is shipped out of these mining areas. Seems that they may be the biggest outlaw of them all."

The conversation was over. Mary knew that arguing

with Charles was as pointless as milking a turnip. She sighed and closed her eyes.

"Mary," Charles said. He rose and helped her to her feet. "I know I'm a disappointment in many ways. It could be said I've spent my life disappointing the people I care most about. In spite of that, I intend to continue down the path I've chosen. It's all I know. I'll be leaving first thing in the morning."

Mary nodded, resisting the urge to say something she couldn't take back. All she cared about anymore was keeping Charles close to her, keeping him safe. And, in spite of what he had chosen to do with his life, she would not walk away from him.

"I know," she said and swept past him. "You've been honest with me, and I have to appreciate that." She turned to glance at him over her shoulder. "Who'd have thought that a thief could be so very honest?"

"Who, indeed?" returned Charles. He followed Mary into the hotel.

Two gentlemen were seated at a small table in the parlor as Charles entered.

"Mr. Bolton," called out one. "I had hoped I'd catch sight of you. I have a few questions to ask. My friend here has purchased some mining interests and, knowing you are a mining expert, I told him you could give him some sound advice."

Charles hesitated before nodding to the stranger. "In truth, I am a poor man to give advice, Henry," he said. "I've just learned that the mines I purchased last year have gone bust. I speculated and lost."

Henry shook his head. "No matter. I know you are a man of character and goodwill. Please, take a seat. We promise not to rob you of more than a little of your time."

Charles shrugged as he looked around. It wouldn't do to display impatience.

192

Mary disappeared into the kitchen, then returned with a tray. She glanced over at him and smiled. A quizzical expression told him she found his predicament amusing.

CHAPTER 58

On August 31, 1881, Charles decided to stop the southbound Roseburg to Redding stage along the Klamath River, about seven miles south of Henley. Selecting a place that was steep and dangerous, Charles knew it would provide protection, just in case tonight's whip was braver than he anticipated. He'd heard about John Sullaway, Yreka's stage driver. A tall man, with a keen eye and sure-fire shotgun at his side, he was not a man to be underestimated.

Charles made a small campfire as a light dusting of snow had fallen and the night was colder than he had expected. He settled in to wait because the nighttime stage would not barrel through until well after midnight.

It was almost 1:30 before Charles heard the thundering of the approaching horses. Quickly he slipped behind some brush and pulled on his flour sack mask. The team had slowed, no doubt after Sullaway spotted the unexpected campfire. With the nearby steep descent down to the river, the driver would not risk endangering his team. He'd take his time.

The moment was perfect.

Charles stepped up to the side of the stagecoach and raised his gun. "Halt!"

Sullaway, surprised by Charles' appearance, cursed loudly, but complied when he spotted Charles' gun. "You can put away the shotgun. I got no quarrel with you."

Charles nodded, his face hidden under his mask and derby. "And I have no intention of hurting you. Not for a thousand dollars," he added. "But I do want the express box and mail pouches, so step down and take hold of your team."

Once more Sullaway complied. "You know," he said, climbing down from the driver's box, "I'm wondering if you're the thief who held up Joe Mason and Nort Eddings last year. You know you may well bankrupt the Yreka Stage Company if you continue to hold us up. Folks don't take kindly to having their stages robbed and mail pouches looted."

"Well," returned Charles as he broke open the strong box, "Wells, Fargo & Company can afford to pay out. The company's a bigger thief than men the likes of me, and unfortunately, I need the money." Wishing the man would shut up, he kept his eye on the shotgun near his feet.

However, Sullaway did not attempt to interrupt him. "You're as sly as any outlaw," he said. "Don't think your reputation hasn't spread. Wells, Fargo & Company have detectives on your trail, and I sure wouldn't want to be in your shoes when they catch you. You ever shoot a man?"

"I'm no gunslinger," snapped Charles. "I've never shot nor injured a man yet, intentionally, and don't intend to start. Now, get back up on your seat and be on your way!"

"There'll be hell to pay someday," returned Sullaway. "You better believe it."

Charles didn't respond, but stepped back as the driver started his horses. They disappeared into the darkness in less than a minute, although their pounding hooves could be heard for long after they'd been swallowed up by the night.

Still irritated by the man's gutsy retorts, Charles pulled off his hat and mask and stuffed them inside his small satchel, then set off at a fast pace. He knew that Sullaway would bring back a posse as soon as he reached Yreka, so time was of the essence. He'd have to take a longer way down to Shasta Valley.

Stumbling over a rock pile, Charles righted himself. "Perhaps I have begun pushing my luck," he said out loud, suddenly unnerved by the events of the night. And perhaps

Mary was right: returning to Siskiyou County had been a poor choice.

On the bright side, he had made a handsome profit, and that had to account for something.

CHAPTER 59

"His days are numbered." James Hume, flipping through the pages of his report, turned to one of his associates. "And before this is over, Black Bart will have the Devil to pay."

"Yes, but you have to admit, this fellow is as cunning as any we've ever dealt with."

"Perhaps," returned Hume, "but poet or not, he's still a common thief. The fact that he enjoys teasing us along the way means little in the long run." He picked up the scraps of paper containing the last two poems left by Black Bart. Selecting one, he read aloud: "Lo, here I've stood, while wind and rain have set the trees a-sobbin'; And risked my life for that damned stage that wasn't worth the robbin'." He frowned. "That every stage would be loaded with a dozen deputies and their six-shooters," he said.

"Well, with these heavier express boxes bolted to the box, he'll have a harder time breaking in. And now that we know more about his identity, it's more'n likely that someone will spot him."

"His description all but matches half the men in California, including mine. But the man travels only on foot, so he can't outrun us forever." Hume picked up the second poem, the last one they'd collected: "Goodbye Shasta County, I will bid you adieu. I may emigrate to Hell, but I'll never come back to you."

"You think he means it? Hasn't he hit that county five times already? Seems he's done okay there."

Hume growled. "He's hit Shasta six times. The last

time was in September '82. The driver was Horace Williams, the same whip Bart held up in October of '81."

"Bet he was mad as a hornet."

"No doubt, but Bart had to be madder still. He didn't make more than a dollar for his efforts." Hume smiled. There was little that tickled his funny bone, but knowing that the road agent had come up dry pleased him.

"That's at least some justice."

Hume frowned. "Not nearly justice," he said. And after Bart's last string of robberies, now numbering well over twenty, he'd determined he'd use any means possible to trap him. The man had fouled Wells, Fargo & Company express for the last time, if he had anything to say about it.

He took out two sheets of foolscap and scrawled a half dozen lines on each, then turned to his colleague. "I want this message telegraphed to every sheriff from here to hell and back. You got it? The reward's been raised so perhaps we'll get someone to talk. Too many fools seem infatuated with this scoundrel. And send this to Harry Morse. He's got as good a sniffer as any man I know. We're putting him on the trail. I promise you, Black Bart will be caught before the year is out. I'll not be made a fool of any longer."

CHAPTER 60

"I will be back in time for Thanksgiving supper." Charles, donning his long coat, smiled at Mary from across the room. He knew she wasn't pleased. She had started in on his quitting again, and he'd tried to appease her with promises to do so, come the new year.

"You've managed to escape capture, for what, seven years now, Charles? Your luck cannot hold out much longer. That Wells, Fargo & Company detective, Hume, has been here, along with half a dozen deputies. They've put out a good reward for you, one I suspect is more than you've managed to make on many of your holdups."

Charles ignored the barb. He knew Mary was concerned about his avoiding capture, but with the success he'd achieved, she had to know he'd outwit them all—any time he had a mind to.

He carefully placed his derby on his head and tapped the brim. "Mary, my dear, trust me. I have managed to keep ahead of even their best leatherheads, including J.B. Hume. He is quite a hound and I must give him his due, but they cannot know when and where I will strike next and they haven't the numbers to send out men in every direction. What if I promise to make this my last strike?"

"Forever, Charles?"

She knew him too well. He smiled. "You know I cannot make such promises. I have prided myself on being a man of my word."

Mary bristled. "Seems to me, in retrospect, you've broken some important promises along the way. Didn't you leave a wife you promised to care for until death do you part? And what about your daughters? Do you think they wonder about how sincere you are?"

Charles said nothing, but he felt a rush of anger. It wasn't like Mary to bring up his past life. He held her stony gaze for a moment longer, then turned away.

He suspected there was more to this outburst than just his thieving.

Indeed, he knew it grieved her more than she was willing to admit, that they couldn't be married. In spite of her reassurances. After all, what woman wanted to remain attached without some kind of legal contract?

Her voice softened. "I know, I promised never to complain. It's just that—"

He held up a gloved hand. "Do not apologize. I have given you plenty of reason to complain. It's a wonder you've put up with me this long."

Mary rushed to him. "Put up with you? Oh, Charley, I'd put up with more if it meant I didn't have to say good-bye."

He chuckled. "You are not only beautiful, you are a stalwart companion. It grieves me to leave you."

She wrapped her arms around him hungrily. "Then don't go. At least, not yet."

"Mary, I must. I'm catching the stage and it rarely comes late. Helm is one of the best whips around."

Mary raised her brows. "I imagine so. Wasn't it he that tripped you up last summer when you attempted a holdup?"

Charles laughed. "Indeed, he and his messenger, George Hackett. George took the hat right off my head."

"He also left some buckshot in your hide," returned Mary.

"So he did. So he did. Still in all, I'm a bit too much polecat, even for them."

CHAPTER 61

It had been well over a year since Charles had held up a Wells, Fargo & Company express stage in Sonoma County, thus he suspected he'd have an easier time of it today. Situating himself at a bend along Geyser Road, about five miles from Cloverdale, he knew he had the advantage. He donned his well-worn mask and linen duster.

A short time later, he hailed the approaching S.V. & C. L. stage, which was traveling at an easy pace. Stepping out, he pressed his shotgun to his shoulder. The horses, frightened, drew back and the driver brought them to a nervous halt.

The driver knew he had no choice but to throw down the treasure box. It landed at Charles' feet with a heavy thud.

"Mail pouches, too," said Charles.

The messenger seated alongside the driver complied. The bags landed atop the express box. Charles nodded, noting they were at least more than half full.

Not wanting to give the driver or express messenger any advantage, he waved them on. As the stage moved past him, he realized there were a number of passengers on board. One young man leaned forward, then quickly pulled his head back inside.

Charles sliced the bags open and smashed the lock on the express box, then stuffed as much of the contents into the small valise he'd brought with him. In minutes he was making his way along the ridge and back the way he'd come.

Not wanting to test Fate, he avoided the Tyler Road House and the Matt Lea Place, as well as Lakeport and all other points where he might encounter people. Instead he pressed on, jogging downhill or across open stretches. He didn't stop, not even for water.

Indeed, hadn't he promised Mary he'd return to Woodville by Thanksgiving?

Later, Charles learned that another well-known road agent, Buck English, had been credited with the holdup. Wells, Fargo Detective Charles Aull had put out the word that English, recently released from San Quentin, had returned to Middletown, in Lake County, only 18 miles from the site of the holdup.

Charles teased Mary. "Didn't I tell you? You must admit I was right as a trivet. They've gone off on another goose hunt. No doubt English himself is snarling about now."

Mary stiffened. "I don't think your managing to escape notice this time is anything to crow about, Charles. It gives me no satisfaction knowing you consider yourself beyond their grasp."

Charles nodded. "True enough. But come, dinner will not wait. Cook has prepared oyster dressing and ordered me to fetch you before her potatoes get lumpy and the gravy turns cold."

With a grim expression, Mary took his arm. She was not happy, that much was clear, but her displeasure was not enough to dispel his own relief that once more he'd escaped Hume and his band of hounds.

CHAPTER 62

James Hume looked over the circular he'd sent out to every Wells, Fargo & Company express agent in northern California and southern Oregon. He motioned to his associate, Jon Thacker. "If it were possible, I'd raise the reward money from $800 to $5000. This thief has made fools of everyone, from here to Jacksonville. It's going to give me great satisfaction to catch him."

Thacker nodded. "There isn't a judge in the region who wouldn't love to convict him. But he's a wily fellow."

"Every man meets his match someday, and someday is coming soon. With Harry Morse's nose and gall, we ought to come up with our man very soon."

"I sure wouldn't want Harry Morse on my trail."

"Neither would I," remarked Hume. "The man has no fear. Look at the way he dealt with the Narcisco Bojorques gang and Juan Soto, one of the deadliest men in California. He never flinched, even when he took him on, face-to-face."

"They say he's not afraid of anyone or anything."

"I don't doubt it."

"He ought to be able to corner Black Bart eventually."

"Well, if we don't capture Black Bart soon, Mr. Valentine may extend the embargo on gold shipments all over the region. He's already placed embargoes on some of the towns in El Dorado and Placer Counties."

As he left his office, Hume had to admit that with each passing day and week, he left the agency more and more agitated. He had hoped to have Black Bart cornered by

Christmas, yet here it was, the summer of 1883 and Bart had not only evaded him, he had managed to stop two more stages in the last six months.

First the Lakeport to Cloverdale stage in April, which had to be no less than his fourth robbery in Sonoma County, and then the stage near Jackson, in Amador County, in June. To his knowledge, Bart had never held up any Amador stages, but that only proved that the man was growing more desperate or more daring. Hopefully, it would also make him more careless.

Interestingly, in Amador, the driver, Clint Radcliffe, found some odd items abandoned at the holdup site: an axe, a hat, a ragged pair of pants, a mask, even some fabric from a woman's dress.

Hume could only hope that the items would provide more clues to Bart's whereabouts. The scraps of information collected so far amounted to little more than hearsay. And the fact that some citizens relished Bart's adventures, comparing him to Robin Hood, was fodder to fuel any lawman's fire.

Hume detested such fabrication of the truth.

Black Bart was nothing more than a two-bit bandit, a man so full of conceit that he enjoyed the titillation of leaving behind bits of verse, something to taunt and tease authorities. In Hume's estimation, this reprobate had managed to evade capture for too long. His outlaw days were numbered.

On the heels of his last robbery to Sonoma County, Hume and Thacker had followed Bart's tracks for many miles, but to no avail. Several locals did note a man, well-dressed and gentlemanly, however, appearing in town from almost nowhere, and the day before the holdup the same man had stopped to ask directions from several residents, even sitting down to a meal with a family and two other travelers at a stage stop. The man had been dressed in a worn, but clean suit and spoke softly. Certainly not one's notion of a notorious stage bandit.

But the description was familiar and reminded Hume that back in 1880 he'd collected a similar description of a stranger passing through Mendocino County. Mrs. Sydney McCreary and her daughter, who lived in Potter Valley, had served dinner to a man so genteel, they'd assumed he was a preacher. But after two robberies were committed near Ukiah, less than sixteen hours and 20 miles apart, Mrs. McCreary, a God-fearing woman, had wondered if the man was any kind of preacher at all.

Mrs. McCreary had also recalled that the man's coat was in need of repair and his shoes were well-worn and split. She had provided a physical description of him: a man of medium build, with blue eyes and graying hair, heavy eyebrows and a nearly white moustache, with slightly receding hairline and at least two teeth missing.

His description had now been confirmed, which gave Hume a stronger sense of Bart's personality; indeed the bandit had to be a master of disguise and deceit.

But Thacker was right; unfortunately Black Bart was also a wily fellow.

CHAPTER 63

Charles awoke, perspiration lining his brow. Impatiently he threw off his blanket and sat up, almost dizzy from the strange dream that had disturbed his sleep.

He had never been prone to nightmares, but lately, he'd suffered through several. He frowned. Mary's persistent admonitions had no doubt affected him. She'd grown so fearful that he'd returned to San Francisco more than two days early, unable to tolerate her outbursts.

He stood up and walked to the window. Outside the San Francisco landscape was shrouded in fog, so dense it felt as if the sky had fallen in on him.

He scanned the dark alley below. Through his paper-thin windows, he could hear, but not see, men moving down the rocky lane. More than likely, they were drunk; on Saturday nights, most men were busy spending every dime on cheap whisky and cheap women.

Glancing at his watch, Charles noted the time: 4:30 a.m. Disgusted that he'd wakened, he returned to his bed, but rather than crawling into it, he picked up the satchel he kept nearby and placed it on the bed.

Again he thought of Mary. He should have known that, just like Mary Elizabeth, she'd ultimately find his choices intolerable.

He rummaged through the pine cupboard where he kept his work clothes as well as his finer togs. He pulled out his linen duster, the costume he used in his holdups, several freshly laundered handkerchiefs, and his derby.

He wasted no time in getting ready; after all, he had

business to tend to. He was going to return to Calaveras County, to the very site where, in July of 1875, he'd held up his first stage. He'd not returned to the spot in eight years, but he was determined to prove to Mary, if not to himself, that he could go and come as he pleased, and that no one, not Hume or Thacker or Morse, could stop him.

It was late October and the weather was balmy in the foothills. Charles stopped first in Tuttletown, then walked the Sonora-Milton stage road to the outskirts of Copperopolis. There he spent the night at the Reynolds Ferry Hotel, a small hotel and stage station near the Stanislaus River. It was run by Signora Rolleri and her many children, including her youngest son, Jimmy.

Jimmy Rolleri not only helped around the hotel, he also ran the ferry that carried the stages back and forth across the river.

"You from 'round here?" asked Jimmy that night at dinner.

Charles hesitated, then said, "I'm up from Bostwick's Bar."

"Ah," said Jimmy. "Have you had any luck down there?"

"Not much," returned Charles with a smile. "Decided to try my luck further upstream."

"Lots of miners come through here," said Jimmy. "Not many of them have more than a little gold dust in their poke."

"Is that so?" Charles smiled. The boy was obviously a keen observer of people, and that suddenly made him nervous. He excused himself abruptly. "Thank you, Mrs. Rolleri. The dinner was lovely, but if you don't mind, I think I'll retire for the evening."

Early the next morning, Charles slipped out of the hotel

207

and made his way to the small grocery store in town.

"Good morning," greeted the smiling middle-aged clerk.

"It is a good morning," Charles said, hoping to avoid any conversation. "I need a few supplies."

"Of course," said the woman, still smiling. "What can I get you?"

"Let me have some of those crackers," he said, pointing to the shelf behind her. "And some sugar."

"Is that all?"

"Yes, for now," said Charles.

CHAPTER 64

Charles examined the Funk Hill grade and smiled. Yes, this was the best site for a holdup and the same spot he'd chosen for his first robbery eight years before. The years had not dimmed his recollection of that initial event nor the thrill he'd experienced after successfully stopping John Shine's stage. The driver had been furious, and rightfully so, thought Charles. He'd been outwitted and overtaken by a single man in a flour sack mask and linen duster.

Reliving the events filled him with anticipation. That he'd chosen this spot again could only prove that he, Charles E. Boles, was a master of his craft. Indeed, no other bandit had succeeded in holding up as many stages as he had. Hadn't he become Wells, Fargo & Company's greatest nemesis? He chuckled. It would be a great laugh to take the same stage a second time.

As night eased into morning, he took up a position beside the lava-capped ridge at the top of the grade and settled in for the long wait. He removed an apple he'd packed and sipped water he'd carried up from the Stanislaus River. The stage would come through sometime after 6:00 a.m., just before sunrise.

Letting his head rest against the stony fortress, he was startled when he heard the sound of two men talking loudly, in addition to the sound of a team of horses moving up the grade.

He turned and pressed himself against the rock. He could not discern the movement of one of the men, but knew that he had climbed off the stage.

He donned his mask and grabbed his gun, then glanced around, the darkness and Manzanita brush preventing him from seeing anything.

Suddenly the stage was nearing the spot he'd selected for his holdup. He ran forward and took a position in the middle of the trail, feet spread, gun pressed to his masked face.

He shouted for the driver to halt, then demanded to know where the man was who had gotten off the stage some 200 or 300 yards earlier.

The driver looked down at him with wide-eyed anger. "It's only a boy, and he's out lookin' for stray cows. He's no threat to you."

Charles glanced around, a sense of foreboding filling him. He turned his gaze back to the driver. "Get down, then, and be quick. Unhitch the team."

"Can't do it," replied the Jehu tersely. "The brake ain't no good. It won't hold."

Charles felt his knees weaken. "Get down anyway. Get a rock."

"Can't do it. You do it if you want to stop this stage."

The moment grew fuzzy in Charles' mind. Should he give up the treasure that he knew lay just beyond his grasp?

He fumbled with his gun, then quickly moved off the trail and grabbed a large stone. Placing it behind the wheel of the stage, he waved the driver down. "Now unhitch them."

The driver moved altogether too slowly. Charles, anxious to get the robbery over, tugged at one of the straps. "Now take them over the hill and stay there 'til I tell you."

The driver complied, but his scowl revealed the depth of his scorn.

After retrieving his sledgehammer from behind the rock, Charles climbed up into the driver's seat and freed the strong box fastened to the boards. Then he tumbled it over the edge along with the mailbags. Glancing around to be sure he was still alone, he jumped down and hacked at the box until he got it opened. He grabbed several bags of gold and shoved them into the mail pouch.

Just then a shot rang out.

Stunned, Charles hesitated. As a second shot was fired, he scrambled for cover behind the rock, dragging the weighted mailbag behind him.

He felt the blood pulsing through his brain. It was impossible to think clearly. One thing was sure: without a loaded weapon, he was helpless. He would have to run for it.

With the heavy bag slung over his shoulder, Charles eased away from his hiding place and started up the hill.

The next shot grazed his hand and Charles spun around, just in time to see a boy with a rifle dash into the trail and take cover behind the abandoned stage. He was clearly a keen rifleman. Charles scurried on, criss-crossing the heavily brushed hillside.

CHAPTER 65

"This is the first worthwhile clue we've had." Harry Morse picked up the handkerchief and turned it over in his hand. "If we could locate where he had his laundry done, we could track him down. Don't every laundry have its own mark?"

"Generally speaking, they do," returned James Hume. "I assume, however, that we're talking about more than 100 laundries in the city alone."

Hume and Thacker, along with Sheriff Benjamin Thorn of Calaveras County, riffled through several items that had been recovered from Black Bart's abandoned campsite.

"What about these opera glasses?" asked Thacker. "Think we could trace where he might've purchased these?"

Hume nodded. "Perhaps. At least we know the man frequented the city. Mrs. Rolleri stated that this Charles Bolton looked to be a real gentleman, and her description certainly matches the ones we've gathered heretofore."

"Lucky that Bart, or Bolton, stayed at her hotel."

"Luckier that Jimmy Rolleri accompanied Reason McConnell on his stage that morning," said Thorn. He'd known Jimmy for some time and knew that the boy was quick. That he'd wounded or frightened Black Bart enough for him to leave the scene of the robbery without retrieving his belongings, had been sheer good fortune.

James Hume looked up. "Henry, find out what you can about the local laundries. Few gentlemen do their own laundry. See what you can come up with."

Henry Morse nodded. "I've got some ideas," he said.

"John? I want you and Thorn to sit down and come up with a clear description of this Bolton, something we can wire to every county sheriff. Then beat feet around the city and contact as many police as you can. Remind them of the reward."

Two days later, Morse entered Thomas C. Ware's office and introduced himself. "Are you the proprietor of the California Laundry?"

Ware nodded. "Indeed. How can I help you?"

Henry Morse smiled. "Well, in fact, I am looking for a gentleman, a mining engineer, and I heard that he has information I'm looking for. I'm also a miner."

Ware raised his eyebrows. "And the man's name?"

"Bolton. Charles Bolton."

"Oh, yes, I know him well. In fact, he's just returned to the city. He often stops by in the late afternoon."

"Wonderful," returned Morse. "I'll return later."

"I'll look for you then, Mr. – uh?"

"Hamilton," returned Morse quickly. Hume had cautioned him not to reveal his identity until they had cornered Bolton. "As I said, I'm interested in finding out what Mr. Bolton knows about the northern mining district."

That afternoon, as Henry Morse and Mr. Ware headed down Post Street, Charles Boles came around the corner and nearly ran into them.

214

"Ah, Thomas," Charles said. "I was headed your way."

"And we were coming to see you. Mr. Hamilton has requested an interview."

Charles Boles nodded to Henry Morse. "Sir?"

Morse, noting that Charles was dressed in a new suit and new derby, extended his right hand. "It's a pleasure. I've heard much about your mining experience and have several questions to ask you."

Charles glanced at his friend's smiling face before taking the stranger's hand. "I will try to answer them as best I can."

"Wonderful," returned Morse. "Shall we walk and talk? It's a lovely afternoon."

"If you wish," said Charles.

"You must excuse me," said Ware. "I have work to do. Good day, gentlemen."

"Thank you, Mr. Ware. I am indebted to you," said Henry Morse. "I have wanted to meet Mr. Bolton for some time. In fact," he added, turning back to Charles, "I have a friend who has also heard of your success in the gold fields. If you have time today, Mr. Bolton, I know I could set up a meeting."

Charles hesitated, then smiled and shrugged. "As you wish, Mr. Hamilton. I am flattered. I had no idea I had a reputation."

"Indeed, you are well thought of in many circles," said Henry Morse.

CHAPTER 66

The two men walked on, turning onto Sansome Street after making their way down Bush, Montgomery, and California streets.

Charles glanced at Mr. Hamilton whenever there was a lull in the conversation. His companion was agreeable, yet there was a reserve, an almost calculated calmness about him that was somewhat unnerving.

Mr. Hamilton pointed to the door of the Wells, Fargo & Company's office building. "My friend works here," he said.

Charles nodded but said nothing. Could Mr. Hamilton have any idea of his real identity? Surely it was only a coincidence that his friend worked inside Wells, Fargo & Company.

Following Hamilton up to the second floor, Charles felt his pulse quicken and his heart lurch as he read the name printed on the door: James B. Hume.

Mr. Hamilton ushered him inside. "James," he said, nodding to the pleasant looking man seated behind a desk, "I'd like you to meet Mr. Charles Bolton."

Hume, standing to his full height, gave Charles a steady look. Slowly he extended his right hand. "It's a pleasure."

Charles hoped his nervousness wasn't apparent. He smiled and shook Hume's hand, then smiled.

Hume smiled in return. "No doubt Wells, Fargo & Company has transported gold from your mine. We like to think we provide a service that's trustworthy and secure."

He seemed to hesitate. "Please, won't you sit down, sir."

Charles took a seat on a small straight-backed chair positioned across from Mr. Hume's large and littered desk. The room smelled of tobacco. "Thank you," he said, after a pause. If only to appear less anxious, he leaned his cane against Hume's desk, then removed his derby and placed it in his lap.

Both Hamilton and Hume seemed to take a particular interest in his hat.

"Our aim is to preserve the trust that patrons put in our stage lines," continued Hume suddenly. "Of course, we all suffer when there's an assault on one of our transports." He lowered himself into his chair, then leaned forward, his gaze clear and demanding.

"Indeed," returned Charles. He turned to Mr. Hamilton. "You said there was a question you had about my mines?"

"Oh, yes," returned Mr. Hamilton. "I understand your mines are in the Mother Lode?"

Charles cleared his throat. "Actually, my principal mine, which produces more silver than gold, is near the California-Nevada line."

"Hmmm," interrupted Hume, "I could have sworn we were told your mining interests lay in the Mother Lode."

"I don't understand," returned Charles sharply, "what difference it makes. I have a number of interests in various locations. You have yet to ask me a question which I can answer."

"Please, bear with us," said Hume. He seemed distracted for a moment as he ruffled through some papers. "I do have a question or two which I believe only you can answer."

Charles fumbled with his derby.

Mr. Hamilton pointed to Charles' left hand. "I see you've injured yourself."

Charles looked down at the shallow cut that ran along

217

the knuckles.

"How did you injure your hand?" asked Hume. The friendliness he'd displayed earlier had been suddenly replaced by a chilly firmness.

"I hardly remember," said Charles. "I believe it was on the train on a trip to Truckee, just recently."

"And is that where your mine is located?" returned Hume, his brows pinched in serious consideration.

Charles stammered, "Gentlemen, what do these questions have to do with anything? I'm certainly not about to discuss my personal business interests with you. I think this conversation is at an end. If you'll excuse me?" He reached for his cane.

"Ah, Mr. Bolton, do you have something to hide? Certainly a businessman of such repute has no reason for concealing the location of one of his mines." Mr. Hume suddenly smiled. "If, indeed, you are Mr. Charles Bolton?"

Charles refrained from jumping to his feet and running from the room. "I don't understand, sir. What are you implying?"

"Sir, I am not one to deceive, but I am a persistent man and determined to ascertain the truth. And the truth is, sir, we believe you are a man with a secret."

Charles stood up, his heart pounding. "You, sir, are out of line!"

Hume jumped to his feet, his voice soft but stern. "Perhaps. Perhaps. But Captain Stone will be in shortly, and along with Detective Morse, the man you know as Mr. Hamilton, and myself, I think we'll accompany you to your room at the Webb House. You are under arrest, Mr. Bolton."

CHAPTER 67

When Charles, accompanied by Sheriff Thorn, Captain Stone, and Detective Morse, reached Stockton, a crowd was waiting at the dock. Many called out to him as if greeting a long lost friend.

Charles nodded to those closest. "Looks like the whole town's here to greet me."

Morse frowned. "I take it Sheriff Thorn didn't heed Hume's warning and keep our arrival quiet."

Captain Stone glanced around at the eager faces. "You're quite famous in these parts," he said to Charles. To Morse he added, "Hume's friends at the Examiner will be furious. They'll have wanted the headline."

"Absolutely," said Morse. "They resent his tendency to ignore them."

Charles smiled in spite of himself. Hume was as strong-minded a man as he'd ever met. But thankfully, Charles had managed to evade many of his questions, and he'd not confessed to anything, although the detectives did locate the handkerchief he'd dropped after the precocious boy shot him, as well as the disguise he'd used many times after escorting him to the Webb House.

But they'd have to collect more evidence if they hoped to pin any other robbery on him. Doing that would not be easy.

Fourteen hours later, as the party of men arrived at the San Andreas jail, Detective Morse interrogated him again.

He presented Charles with an assortment of evidence he and Hume had collected over the last couple of years, including a Mrs. Crawford's description of him and Reason McConnell's recognition of his voice. Morse had somehow located a writing sample, to boot, and when compared to the flimsy bit of verse Charles had left after one of his holdups, the scrawl proved to be quite similar.

"A full confession could make the difference between a light sentence and a maximum sentence," explained Morse, "and spare everyone a long or tedious trial."

Stone agreed. "It behooves a gentleman to admit his crimes and perhaps even make restitution."

Charles hesitated. "But gentleman, I cannot answer to such crimes. If I did, perhaps I'd have to confess to war crimes, too. As you recall, I served my country nobly during the war, a war many considered to be criminal." He played with the narrow brim of his natty new derby. "What purpose would that serve?"

"Please, Mr. Bolton, do not think us dim-witted," snapped Stone. "We have sufficient evidence to lock you up for any number of years. Good sense would ease your trouble."

"So, a full confession might keep such a man out of jail?"

Morse chuckled. "The law does not look upon any stage robbery lightly, Mr. Bolton. There would have to be a prison sentence. How could any judge do otherwise? He'd more'n likely end up at the end of a rope himself."

"My dear Mr. Morse, I was speaking hypothetically. As I said earlier, I have not nor will I confess to such a host of crimes as you've outlined. Why, it'd be tantamount to slipping a noose around my neck."

"Ah, I suspect there are no less than a dozen men who would eagerly slip that noose around your throat. Mr. Hume, for one."

Charles smiled. Morse was a staunchly honest fellow.

221

"He is persistent, isn't he? Such an admirable trait."

"Mr. James Hume is the most determined man I've ever known. He's a match for anyone."

"Indeed," returned Charles, with a smile. "Indeed."

CHAPTER 68

The case against Charles Bolton, a.k.a. Charles E. Boles, a.k.a. Black Bart, was heard on November 16, 1883, by Judge P. H. Kean, in San Andreas, California.

Charles entered a plea of "guilty" for robbing the Sonora-Milton stage on Funk Hill on November 3. He refused to admit involvement in any other holdup.

The following day, after waiving his right to a jury trial, Charles again pleaded guilty before Superior Judge C. V. Gottschalk. Once more he admitted that he'd robbed the Funk Hill stage, but once more he refused to consider any other charges.

The judge, frustrated that nothing more could be proved, sentenced him to six years in San Quentin Prison.

Charles held his breath. He could have received a stiffer penalty. He was relieved.

It was over. All over. He'd be going to San Quentin.

And he'd not even had a chance to contact Mary. Surely she'd read the headlines already. Would she contact him? Or would she leave him to his just desserts and forget she'd ever dallied with him?

And what about his family? The headlines would be sent all over the East, no doubt. The infamous Black Bart: Caught! Identity REVEALED?

Back in his cell, Charles asked the jailer for pen and paper. "I have some letters I must write," he said. "My family has not heard from me in almost 15 years."

"Yeah, well, they probably don't care to hear from you

now, neither," chuckled the jailer. "You ain't nothin' to brag about, that's for sure. But I'll ask the sheriff."

Charles refrained from any response. He only hoped his request would not be denied. The image of his photograph being sent all over the East suddenly filled him with shame. His daughters. Mary Elizabeth. Sarah and John. Robert and Hiram and the rest of his family.

Thankfully, both Mother and Father were gone now. Let them rest in peace.

When the jailer returned an hour later, he brought several slips of writing paper, rather dull in quality, and a broken scrap of pen and half-filled bottle of ink. "The best I could find," explained the jailer. "Nobody seemed to care much whether you wrote your family. I suspect they already learned the truth 'bout your sentence and all."

"Thank you."

But it was almost impossible to find the words he needed. He wrote Mary first, a letter full of apologies and promises. Would she even read it?

Next he wrote Mary Elizabeth. Could she ever forgive him? And the girls? Would they continue to think of him as dead? How old would they be now? Were any of them married or betrothed? In the end, did it matter? He'd abandoned them all. He'd forfeited any right to be forgiven.

Disgusted by his own arrogance, he nearly tore up the letters, then resisted.

He'd not be given many chances in the future to contact his family once he was inside San Quentin. And six years at his age could be just about all he'd have left in life.

He threw the pen across the floor. He'd have done well to listen to Mary before their final parting. He'd have done well to heed Mary Elizabeth's pleas to live a good life. Even his mother's ominous words haunted him now: "Charles, life to you is about taking risks and seeking adventure. And someday you'll have to pay the piper."

CHAPTER 69

"San Quentin
Dec. 20th '83

Mr. H. G. Boles,

Yes, 'tis only <u>too true</u>.
I am your brother
lost in disgrace
let this suffice for
the present—

Your once loved brother
C. E. Boles"

Charles folded the letter carefully. What more could he say? Hiram was going to be very disappointed; he'd always been so even-tempered. Not like Father. Not like Robert. Not even like David.

Still in all, it was Mary Elizabeth and the girls who would suffer the most after Charles' debacle, and he owed them a full explanation. He owed them more than that, but he was incapable of providing anything more.

He wasn't even sure of their whereabouts. The last letter he'd had from Sarah and John had come many years before. Apparently Mary Elizabeth had sold their property in New Oregon, packed the girls up and returned to Illinois, then moved on to Hannibal, Missouri, where Mary Elizabeth had became a seamstress and at least one of the girls was betrothed.

Charles called for the prison jailer, Captain Aull. "Post this letter, please?"

"It'll have to go through Warden Shirley first. But there shouldn't be a problem."

Charles was grateful that the warden had turned out to be courteous, even, at times, amused by the stories surrounding Charles' daring escapades. Of course, Charles would never confess to any of the long list of robberies now attributed to him, for he knew that James Hume and Wells Fargo & Company would pursue further judgment against him.

Six years already loomed like a life sentence.

Charles took out another sheet of paper and scribbled a few lines to Mary at the Woodville Hotel. She'd not yet made the trip to San Quentin and that worried him. Would she ever forgive him? He'd had only one visitor so far, an old acquaintance from the 116th Illinois Volunteers who lived north of San Francisco. That had been a surprise and a delight.

It took a few months before Charles received a letter from Mary Elizabeth and the girls, and it came in care of Wells Fargo & Co., Inc. His wife's warm and familiar greeting surprised him as did her assurance that she would anxiously await her husband's release. She added that the girls would surely forgive him, now that they knew he was alive.

Stunned, Charles reread the heartfelt missile. Mary Elizabeth's fealty and kindness was like a tonic to his weary and battered mind. Perhaps he'd given up too soon on their marriage; perhaps he should have returned home after coming up bust in Montana back in 1871.

But that was so long ago, it was useless to bemoan his loss.

One afternoon, Captain Aull appeared at Charles' cell and held out two more letters, one from Mary Elizabeth, the other from his youngest daughter. He admonished him, saying, "Charles, your wife is a good woman to stand by you after such abominable treatment. You'd do well to return her a good and kindly report, even if, in the end, you cannot fulfill your marriage promises to her."

Charles knew the captain was right. Besides, if Mary never returned, perhaps he should go back to Mary Elizabeth and the girls.

It was the next day before he sat down and penned a letter:

"November 10, 1884

My dear & loving family,

I wrote last night but failed to send it as useless & now feel in a different mood consequently I will try again & I will start by thanking you for all your loving letters & telling you of my getting a good loving letter today from our darling Baby (Frances Lillian) & I was very glad to hear of her good health & she sent me HGB's (Hiram's) letter to you also...

I have just come from Supper. Had Soup, veal, Milk, Bread, Butter, Roast beef, Squash fried & boiled Potatoes, Pickles, Macaroni & a nice dish of bread Pudding to wind up on & this is our usual bill of fare & same thing Sundays. And when the gas is turned on it almost makes me think of being in town at a regular Restaurant & do you not think I appreciate it to the fullest extent & perhaps you would be surprised to know that I wear the Same Clothes that you saw me in My Photo or nearly so. The same coat, vest, Hat, Shirts, Collars, Cuffs but Prison Pants, but they would never attract the least attention anywhere only where the people are accustomed to seeing them on Prisoners ...Yes My dear family I am wearing the very identical Laundry Mark on My Shirts Collars & Cuffs every day that led to My Capture & imprisonment & this is a facsimile of it Fxo7. That simple little thing Changed me from a respectable honored Citizen, to a Notorious outlaw and villain in the twinkling of an eye in the estimation of the people...

My own dear family, I am very proud of you when I think of your heroic exertions in this cold world in support of each other & I love you more ever letter I read from you for I discover new beauties of character & nobleness in every one of your affectionate letters to me. They are so transparent, I mean beautifully transparent because I can see so clearly & distinctly all the beautiful attributes necessary to constitute a loving noble kind & affectionate woman. So mindful of the welfare of her dear mama & her sweet sister. So little self & such a great big warm heart for others. How I hope she may be fortunate in the Selection of a Companion for life & have the protection of a Man worthy of her affections. Eva & Ida don't be jealous. The language would apply with equal force to either of you. I must close so goodnight.

C. E. B."

CHAPTER 70

Mary came to him on a windy and wet afternoon, nearly three years after he'd been imprisoned. Charles was stunned when he received the note announcing her arrival.

Captain Aull led him down a damp and dark corridor to the small room reserved for visitation. He waited impatiently, then smiled when he saw her enter, elegantly gloved and dressed in a wool cape that trailed across the floorboards like an expensive gown. Her long hair had been threaded with brightly colored ribbons, and her face flushed in anticipation under the sheer veil of her bonnet.

"I don't believe it," he whispered.

"Oh, how could you not?" she chided, lowering herself into the chair beside the table where Charles stood. "Sit. Sit."

Charles plopped down, feeling more like a schoolboy than a man of 56.

Mary untied her cloak but kept it around her shoulders. "It's cold in here."

"Not as cold as a cell," he said. "Or as cold as nights spent dreaming of you."

Mary glanced around the empty room. "I've missed you."

"I've despaired over not seeing you," returned Charles. "I was sure you'd turned from loving me to despising me."

"My wonderful foolish Charley. I knew from the start that our love affair would be one for the poets."

His heart lurched. "Then why did you wait so long to come to me?"

She shrugged, her eyes narrowed but twinkling. "Perhaps to punish you for leaving me all alone. These last three years have been almost intolerable, you know. I moved away from the hotel, but even still, those who knew about us harass me as often as they're able."

"What about?"

Mary chuckled, revealing fine lines around her eyes. "Oh, Charles, about you. You have inspired tall tales and songs, even a stage show or two. Black Bart, the PO8. Just this year I've had a half dozen reporters ask for the truth behind the enigmatic bandit who left bits of verse along the trail."

Charles laughed. "What a trifling bother over nothing. I'm hardly worth the notoriety. And my poetry is worth even less."

Mary slid her gloved hand across the table. Charles leaned forward and gently stroked the tips of her fingers. She sighed audibly. He smiled.

"You're not a bother," she said, "but I've not stopped worrying since your capture. My sis thinks I should walk away and never return. Only it's too late. I have loved you for too long and cannot imagine life without you."

"I didn't know how I was going to face my release if I couldn't have you," said Charles, suddenly sure that any notion of returning to his wife was as ridiculous now as it had been twenty years ago.

Mary whispered, "I've started saving money and have built a tidy little nest egg already."

"But I won't be released for another three years."

"Which will give me more time to come up with a plan. We're going to leave California and never return. Maybe we should sail to the Orient. Or down to Mexico. Where doesn't matter."

Charles glimpsed the anxiety that suddenly seemed reflected in her eyes. The last three years had done their damage. "Where does not matter, is right. You are my greatest treasure, Mary," he said. "I want to spend the rest of my days with you."

"You shall, sir, you shall, or I shall run you through with your own ebony cane."

Charles chuckled, wishing he could put his arms around her.

"Now, I must take my leave. The dampness is settling in my bones."

"Please write, Mary," said Charles, leaning forward. "Letters are all the communication I have with the outside world."

Mary touched her fingers to her lips and nodded. "I'll write soon."

After Mary left, Charles was led back to his cell.

"She's quite a beauty," said Captain Aull as he closed the cold iron door behind him.

Charles said nothing, only sat down on the cot that lined the far wall. The dim, hollow chamber seemed to echo the strange emptiness that now filled him. He glanced over at the water-stained wall opposite and studied the ragged words scratched into the plaster by those who'd come before him.

Phantoms, every one.

And until today, he'd considered himself a phantom, as well. After all, he probably didn't have the right to expect more out of life.

On the other hand, maybe no one had the right to expect much in this convoluted world. Look at David. At Arian. At Henry or Lewis or Castor.

He pushed the anguish of their lives aside. He couldn't take up the past or he'd be lost, and he'd spent far too many years trying to outrun their misery.

So how could he feel such—hope?

He took a slow deep breath and closed his eyes. The scent of Mary clung to him and he knew that there was no turning back.

Mary was what he wanted. She was the rock upon which his final years would be built, the cornerstone to whatever world was open to him. Apart from David, she had turned out to be the one who loved him in spite of his failings. She would not expect him to apologize for who or what he was, or for who and what he'd become.

Suddenly the small square cell seemed to dissolve, and rather than feeling trapped, he felt free.

Life, after all, had revealed its hidden treasure.

EPILOGUE

Charles E. Boles, prisoner #11046, was paroled from San Quentin on January 21, 1888, having served 4 1/2 of his 6-year prison term. He was given his personal belongings and $5.00, wished well by the new warden, McComb, and released. He agreed to a brief news conference and responded to the journalists' probing with humor and familiarity, but he never provided complete answers to any of the questions so many longed to have answered.

The day after his release, a personal ad was placed in the San Francisco Examiner. It read: "Black Bart WILL HEAR SOMETHING to his advantage by sending his address to M. R. Box 29, this office." Who placed the ad and what became of any encounter has never been revealed. Was it a reporter, perhaps Randolph Hearst, who hoped to capture the final and real story of the elusive highwayman? Was it one of the many theater groups who hoped to turn his story into a melodrama? Or was it someone in his family who hoped to contact him? It's anybody's guess.

Ten days following his release, Charles wrote the first of several letters to his wife, Mary Elizabeth Boles:

"My dear loving Wife and Children: After waiting all these days hoping to be able to comply with your wishes and my own most ardent desires, I most sincerely regret that I MUST disappoint you. My dear it is UTTERLY impossible for me to come now, O my constant loving Mary and my darling children, I did hope and I had good reason for hoping to be able to come to you and end this terrible terrible uncertainty, but it seems that it will end only with my life. Although I am free and in Fair health, I am most miserable.

My Dear family I wish you could give me up for ever & be happy, for I fear I shall be a burden to you as I live no matter where I am. My loving family I would willingly sacrifice my life to enjoy your loving company for a single week as I once was. I fear you will blame me for not coming but Heaven knows it is an utter impossibility."

He continued on, telling them that he had not seen any of his old friends, although many extended the hand of friendship. He asserted that the newspapers ran stories that were toted as interviews but were false. He ended by promising to return home before "next Christmas anyhow and if Possible sooner."

In the next letter to Mary Elizabeth, he bemoaned his relationship with his family that was "as ropes of sand," including a "once loving sister, only a few miles away." In fact, one sister and her family did live at Knight's Landing, California, and there remains, to this day, an empty headstone in the family plot. Some speculate that after Charles' eventual death, he was buried there. Likewise, an empty headstone stands between the gravesites of Mary Elizabeth and Ida Boles (Warren), in the Mt. Olivet Cemetery, Hannibal, Missouri. Was he buried in either place? Dates of his death range from 1891, after Mary Elizabeth Boles listed herself as a "widow", to 1917, after a brief obituary appeared in a New York newspaper.

In the last known letter to Mary Elizabeth, which Mary sent to James Hume, Charles wrote: "My Dear Family how little you know of the terrible ordeal I have passed through, and how few of what the World calls good men are worth the Giant Powder it would take to blow them into eternity…"

He concluded with, "I must close now after telling you again not to worry about me, and all may come out better than I expect, at least I hope so. Now may Heaven bless you and all our loved ones. Good Night. Your unhappy, unworthy husband. C. E. Boles."

Whether Charles actually believed that the law was still after him, no one is sure.

Rumors began to circulate, however, and newspapers, jostling for prominence, wrote up new tales and interviews with Black Bart that were possibly, or probably, fabricated. There were a flurry of new sightings, even new robberies, but all remain—to this day—cloaked in mystery.

So did he return to his life of crime?

Though Charles was suggested as a possible suspect in several later holdups, arguments even then ensued as to the reliability of the claims. Also purported was the notion that Wells, Fargo & Company paid Charles a monthly stipend to stay away from its stages, but that has been refuted by Wells, Fargo & Company for more than a century.

Finally, as to Charles' relationship with Mary Vollmer, his supposed mistress, there is only scant evidence to suggest that their affair was real, although many claim there was a woman to whom he remained devoted during his last years in California. That he visited Woodville Hotel (later renamed Woodleaf), there is no doubt. He was sighted by many in the region and he was liked by most of those with whom he came into contact. There is one story that Charles and Mary left California and settled in Pennsylvania where they lived out their lives. Aside from a family story or two, however—which contradict each other—no one can document what really happened to Charles.

What facts do exist are these:

After his release from San Quentin, Charles E. Boles (a.k.a. Bowles or Bolton) never returned to Mary Elizabeth or the girls, and he disappeared into obscurity sometime in November 1888. One day he was listed as a resident of the Nevada House in San Francisco, and the next day he was gone.

He simply vanished.

As to his family:

Mary Elizabeth Boles worked as a seamstress in Hannibal, Missouri, and died in 1896. She never remarried and she continued to defend her husband's name and reputation until the end.

Ida Boles married, moved to Salt Lake City, reportedly had a daughter, and died at age 43 of consumption. She was buried in Hannibal.

Eva Boles married, became a stenographer, had four children (two died in infancy), and died in Hannibal in 1922.

Lillian became a seamstress, married, had a daughter, and died in Oklahoma in 1929. She was buried in Hannibal.

The remaining family knew little about Charles' separate life. Because there were few original documents or letters, much has been left to speculation.

Included here, however, is a family portrait never seen by anyone outside the family. Located in 2001, the photo was sent by Thelma Farmer, Hiram Boles' granddaughter. Seated in the center are John Boles, Sr., and Maria McCue Boles. Hiram Boles is located third from the right. Though Charles is not identified specifically, Thelma believes he is third from the left.

So, what happened to Charles E. Boles, a.k.a. Charles Bowles, a.k.a. Charles Bolton, a.k.a. Black Bart?

Obviously, he left San Francisco and headed to places where he wouldn't be recognized.

How did he make his living? In truth, though he had been a courageous soldier and was recognized for his leadership and ingenuity, he proved a poor farmer, an average teacher, a moderately successful miner, and an amateur poet.

What he did do best was hold up stages, and to this day he remains the most successful and colorful stage bandit in California history. But if he did rob more stages, there is no clear evidence to document it. There is no clear evidence to suggest otherwise, either.

There is an empty grave in Knight's Landing in a family plot; there were reports that he returned to New York and died in the 1900s; there were also reports that he sailed to Japan or parts unknown.

Truly, the facts are as skewed now as they were one hundred years ago, making Charles' final days as mysterious and elusive as his years as a bandit.

Even now there is a $200 reward for the tangible, credible evidence as to the remaining chapter of Black Bart, the PO-8's life.

ACKNOWLEDGMENTS

The authors would like to acknowledge a number of people who aided in the research and collection of information, from documenting locations to uncovering incidental details about the life of Charles Boles. Though many others have assisted in the research—and it's impossible to identify every individual—the following people provided unique bits of history. Thank you to the following (in alphabetical order): Thomas Anderson; Marian Bianchi; John Boessenecker; John Bowman; Janet Brewer; Joyce Buckland; Lewis and Bernice Disbrow; Thelma Farmer; G. Jenkins; Bob Jernigan; Jim Lague; Debra Leonard; Rosemarie Mossinger; and Florence White. Thank you also to Glenn Harrington and the *PARADISE POST*; Doug Jenner; Desiree Kaae; Sue Legerton; Michele Murphy; and Wells Fargo.

Special thanks to the following institutions: Butte County Public Library, Oroville, California; Wells Fargo Historical Archives; Merriam Library, CSU Chico; U.C. Berkeley's Bancroft Library; Jefferson County Library, Oswego, New York; The California Historical Society; National Archives, Washington, D.C.; The Forsythe, Illinois, Library; Alexandria Bay, NY, Library; Marion County Library in Decatur, Illinois; and The San Francisco Public Library (Main Branch).